The Temple Chronicles- Book 1

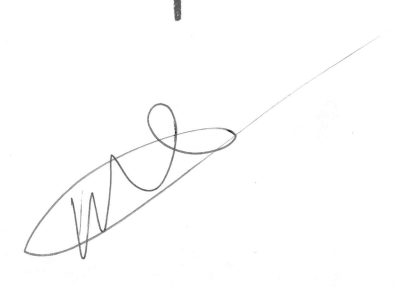

THE JESIAH SCROLLS:

A Story of Worship and Forgiveness in Solomon's Temple

THE JESIAH SCROLLS

ISBN-13: 978-1456324988
ISBN-10: 1456324985

Cover art and design by Sarah Sams (www.sarahsams.com)

Acknowledgements

I would like to thank my family and friends for their support and encouragement during this project. Many long days and nights were spent researching and writing the manuscript—not to mention the seemingly endless editing process. I would also like to especially acknowledge the many people whose heroic assistance throughout the project helped make the book more readable, interesting and relevant. In particular I want to acknowledge my wife Eunice, my children Aubrey, John and Allison, my 'Abba' Corley and Mary Lois, my sister-in-law Kathy Senyard, and good friends Jon and Karen Gindhart, Michael Reid and Rosie and Gregg Alcoke. May God's favor continue to smile on this and related future projects in the Temple Chronicles series.

THE JESIAH SCROLLS

Preface

The Temple Chronicles are a creative series of books, tales, and manuscripts; each uniquely designed to bring the usually dusty and often dry Biblical stage to life— full HD 3D 1080p plasma color for modern readers. Each of the Chronicles is undergirded with well-researched Christian, Jewish and non-religious scholarship— each taking advantage of recent archaeological discoveries and a wide variety of original and secondary documentation and research. Most of the characters are imaginary, though they live in a very historical setting among very historical people and places. The namesake of this book, *Jesiah** lived and worked in the *First Temple* of the great King Solomon, just shortly after its construction and a few years after the *shekinah* glory of Yahweh had entered into the *Holy of Holies*.

Perhaps the reader should be warned at the beginning of the journey. Due to the high standards of Biblical exegesis and scholarly research held to in this project, parts of the books can possibly be a bit daunting. In other words, these books are not necessarily 'light reads'. But don't lose hope. Each book attempts to explore a variety of questions, themes, and cultural topics

* *Note: All italicized words are included in a Glossary (p. 181ff)*

(historic and modern) that are far less scholarly and erudite, and hopefully very interesting and relevant to modern novel readers.

So many historical texts must limit their scope primarily to documented facts about events, places, and people. But through the informed genre of story telling, *The Jesiah Scrolls* can go further than just the facts, and boldly explore the feelings and perceived intentions of the characters. A textbook can describe how worship took place in *Iron Age II High Holy Days*. *The Jesiah Scrolls* can do that as well—but then enter into the heart questions that the faithful might have had as they walked up the many steps to the Temple courts, or watched the scapegoat be released to the Eastern wilderness. *The Jesiah Scrolls* can imagine what worshippers would have felt as the High Priest confessed their annual sins over the chosen sacrifices.

Imagine a Jew coming to the *Day of Atonement* after their life had been wrecked by the intentional betrayal of a colleague, a relational violation that had shattered their world. What could they possibly have hoped to get out of the liturgy? What might their expectations have been on this holy day?

These emotions and questions are not just ancient ones. They are alive and well today in every heart in every church and every synagogue. What are we really supposed to feel as we come into God's holy presence? Do the liturgy and worship make any difference to our lives right now?

Ancient Worship
For Jews and Christians who read this book, you will observe that there are indeed many similarities to modern liturgy and practice; but you will no doubt also be struck by the radical and significant differences.

Why such differences? Think with me. *Jesiah* lived before any Jew could have imagined a Judaism without a temple. He could never have imagined that God would allow His people to go through even one devastating holocaust, much less three (or more). He lived when Israel was a sovereign state ruled by a single King chosen by God, and an heir to so many lavish covenant promises.

6

He lived in a time when God's palpable, visceral *shekinah* glory actually dwelt in the very midst of the people. Pre-exilic Israel was indeed the intimate people of an indwelling personal immanent God.

Judaism today is a product of two diasporas, two temple destructions, centuries of oppression and occupation and many holocausts. Jewish theology has grown up having to openly question God and His goodness. Modern Jewish theology has had to embrace extended exile from the land—only now to have survived 'temple-less' for almost two millennia— and counting. Most importantly, modern Israel has had to survive for almost 2500 years as an orphaned people, absent of God's specific *shekinah* presence.

Ancient Forgiveness and Reconciliation

This book is also about conflict management, broken relationships, crimes of passion, justice, forgiveness and reconciliation of individuals and community all in the shadow of the *High Holy Days*. To say that forgiveness is a huge issue for modern Jews is a vast understatement. There has been so much written on this topic over the last 2000 years— so much disparate dialogue, and in general, forgiveness remains a perennial frustration for God's chosen and tragically beat-up people. By the way, the same failure can be observed in Christian circles. For people who have 'forgiveness' at the very core of their doctrine, followers of the Rabbi Jesus certainly are not well known for prowess in this area.

Don't misunderstand me. Forgiveness, particularly individual-to-individual forgiveness, is central to modern Jewish expressions of the *High Holy Days*. Today the faithful Jews gather annually at their local synagogues to participate in the 10 *Days of Awe* (the period of severe heart due-diligence between *Rosh Hashanah* and *Yom Kippur*) to explore how each has been 'hurt' and how each has been 'hurtful' within the community. It is a time of intentional severe pre-trial due diligence.

7

Though not ancient, a ceremony has been added immediately at the end of the ten days called *Kol Nidrei*:

"I hereby forgive all who have hurt me, all who have done me wrong, whether deliberately or by accident, whether by word or deed. May no one be punished on my account. And I forgive and pardon fully those who have done me wrong. May those whom I have harmed forgive and pardon me, whether I acted deliberately or by accident, whether by word or deed. I am now ready to fulfill the commandment of 'to love my neighbor as myself'."

Though no doubt the words are well meaning and sincere, the experiential repentance and forgiveness may often feel more like the pious hard work of a people still in exile from their God, spiritual orphans, than it arguably might have felt in the shadow of Solomon's temple in the 10th century BCE. It was at the temple where the corporate people of God humbly and helplessly gathered in His visceral presence, expecting to receive a miracle, a redemption by His hand, and to become again a reconciled people and community. There is much that can be learned from *Jesiah* for both Jews and Christians who struggle with forgiveness, and who also struggle with victimization and victimizing alike.

Reader Notes
Apart from this Preface, *The Jesiah Scrolls* is not told in my voice per se, but rather by the story-telling prowess of an imagined author, a Jewish archaeologist/scholar, the son (and namesake) of another imagined Jewish archaeologist/scholar, Dr. Ehud Baruch. This is not exactly a typical authorial 'pen name', a 'nom de plume', or some pseudonym adopted to protect the innocent. Not at all. Rather it is designed to feel like a story actually told by a kosher story-telling *Abba* to his children and family to instruct them in what it means to be a Jew— what it means to be a '*First Temple*' Jew, Dr. Baruch will say. As a story-teller myself, I feel that this shift in narrator is important, because it is after all a very Hebrew story and so should be told by a Jew—even an imaginary one. For me, it is wonderfully appropriate that this would be a Gentile re-

telling of a very Jewish tale of sacrifice and redemption. This is as it should be, Amen!

The reader will be interested to know that the background story of *The Jesiah Scrolls*, the digging of the *'Rabbi's Tunnel'* and subsequent riots are actually historical; though to my awareness, no scrolls were actually found—but who knows?

In order to establish and maintain the feel of Jewish authenticity, I have also chosen to keep language and terms that would have likely been commonplace in an Orthodox Jewish Jerusalem family dialogue, particularly the families of renowned Hebrew archaeologists like Dr. Baruch; but terms that would likely be unfamiliar to many modern Western readers. A glossary has been included for many of the terms, which are noted in italics.

For the stalwarts who make it through the book, it is my hope that the reader will indeed know more about the Temple workings in *Iron Age II* Israel than many modern Jewish and Christian sage wannabes. Perhaps even more important, it is my hope that the reader will have learned important aspects of ancient Biblical forgiveness and reconciliation that will be of great value during their own *High Holy Days*. Imagine being freed at last from the painful and nagging crimes that have shaped one's identity and sense of worth for days, weeks, or even years? At the ancient *First Temple Yom Kippur*, victims could indeed experience real and lasting forgiveness; a forgiveness that is not in any way separate from real justice and consolation. At *Yom Kippur*, victims were invited to a trial before the Judge of the entire Universe for the violation committed against them. Perhaps what makes modern efforts of forgiveness experientially impotent is that they so often overlook 'justice'. The reason that most of us cannot really forgive is that we have not had our day in court yet. Is pre-trial *Kol Nidrei* just well meaning words? I wonder if they would be far more appropriate post-trial? I wonder if a restored liturgy of forgiveness and restoration is ultimately is the real legacy of the *Yom Kippur* of *Jesiah's* tale?

And now the tale within a tale within a tale begins. I would like to introduce you to my newest friend, your host and

9

storyteller, the renowned young Israeli archaeologist, Dr. Ehud Baruch Jr.

Bill Senyard
Golden, Colorado
October 2010

Introduction

By Dr. Ehud Baruch Jr.

This book is being published on the tenth anniversary of my father's death. Perhaps it is best to see this manuscript as less of a book, per se, and more of an homage to the storyteller himself. My '*Abba*', Dr. Ehud Baruch, was an Orthodox Jew and former professor of ancient languages at Hebrew University, one of the leading archaeologists at the Israeli Antiquities Authority. *Abba* was an inspiring, loving husband and father, who was committed to teaching each of his eight sons about our special roots as children of Abraham.

The actual scrolls, upon which this fictional novel is loosely based, have <u>not</u> been published elsewhere in scholarly archaeological journals or lectured on widely. As far as I know, to-date, they have never actually seen the light of day. Officially, the scrolls never existed. But it is fair to say that these same scrolls that never 'existed' and were never officially 'found', radically reshaped my *Abba's* sense of his identity as a Jew—as he would say a *First Temple* Jew. It also shaped *Abba's* understanding of Jewish concepts of forgiveness, justice and reconciliation, something that he intentionally leaned into for the rest of his life. There were many memorable late night discussions about forgiveness with our Rabbi—which unfortunately are beyond the purview of this book.

As my father described the events of that day to us shortly before cancer took his life in mid-1999, his team from the University was on a severe digging schedule at the *Ophel* of the City of David, trying to complete a large section of the dig before the summer temperatures of August became too unbearable. Word of a discovery had come to them from what my *Abba* called a 'surprising source', but he refused to elaborate. He would only say that the information came from a very high level within the government, but he dared not say any more. Apparently, a remarkable cache of scrolls, in amazingly pristine condition, had been 'accidentally' found near the *Western Wall*.

We now know a little better what actually happened. After the Six-Day War in 1967, Orthodox rabbis, who some suggest were under the auspices of the Ministry of Religious Affairs, had begun digging a very illegal tunnel. The entrance to the now named '*Rabbi's Tunnel*' is located near the *Western Wall* plaza (also known as the '*Wailing Wall*') and winds northward along the *Western Wall* of the *Temple Mount* compound. As you can imagine, this presented a very politically provocative situation. The *Western Wall* is all that remains of the original retaining wall for the Great *Second Temple* of King *Herod*, but now houses the holy Muslim shrines of the *Al-Aqsa Mosque* and the *Dome of the Rock*.

But for a few in Jerusalem there are some things more important than international sensitivities. It had long been supposed by some influential members, particularly of the *Chasidim*, that just behind the retaining wall, underneath the current *Temple Mount* was not only tons of rocks, trash, and dirt fill, but ancient holy artifacts strewn among them: gold and brass utensils, pots, candelabras, vessels of the *Second Temple* of Herod— perhaps even the very *Ark of the Covenant* itself. "Old men's desperate dreams," *Abba* would say.

Rumor had it that the rookie archaeologist rabbis worked with some government knowledge, but there was little government oversight. Certainly there were no professional, experienced archaeologists among them. This turned out to be their downfall. As they clumsily tunneled north, the rabbis stumbled upon an underground gate, ancient and sealed, leading eastward to a very crude man-made vault, situated almost directly under the very spot where the *Holy of Holies* would have been. Perhaps it was the loud digging or perhaps the ecstatic Jewish singing and dancing that Muslim temple guards on top of the *Temple Mount* heard that evening through a closed cistern. The 'Rabbi's tunnel affair' caused a huge international furor, complete with violent local riots and confrontations that will not be soon forgotten. Here is how my father told the story, shortly before his passing.

"In the middle of the night, under the cover of the darkness of a moonless summer night sky, my team was led into the highly guarded clandestine tunnel being dug deep under the Jerusalem neighborhoods and markets that exist along the outer side of the *Kotel* (the *Western Wall*). The project was a political nightmare for all involved. Those who ran the very clumsy illegal operation understood the tremendous sensitivity required, for what was formerly the western wall of *Herod's* Temple, and the Holiest of all places on the planet for the Jewish people, is today the retaining wall for the third holiest spot on the planet for all Muslims— many of whom live only 40 feet above the tunnel."

"My team, under great duress and multiple objections, was urgently ordered into the tunnel by the rabbis and armed guards (the latter provided for our own protection I suspect now—but then we did not feel so safe), but were told nothing of what was happening. The rabbis led us through the maze of amateurishly quarried tunnels in a generally northward direction. You can imagine our great surprise when we came to the 'accidental' eastward facing breech in-between two of the gigantic Temple foundation stones. It took our breath away; we knew the implications of what we were looking at. This was holy ground, and for archaeologists, holier still— the stuff that dreams are made of. We were about to enter Jewish history, a man-made vault, at least 2000 years old, underneath the heart of the Temple Mount."

13

THE JESIAH SCROLLS

"As I looked into the opening, the light from my excavation helmet shining into the void, it appeared that the tunnel was only large enough for a single person to enter at a time. We needed to be very careful. Not only was the tunnel ancient and quite deteriorated, but also there was no sign of any support beams or load bearing structures. But we were archaeologists; this is what we do. Nothing was going to keep any of us from proceeding further, neither politics, nor the possibility of tunnel implosion. We carefully entered the ancient tunnel, our hearts racing, and proceeded a very short distance until the tunnel opened up. We found ourselves in a vault packed with scrolls and a variety of instruments and paraphernalia in surprisingly good condition. We had little time to consider the enormity of this find, for we had been given strict orders from the highest level of government that this vault needed to be emptied immediately, without delay, without even cataloguing the find. Pictures were taken, but I have never seen them and I suspect that they were destroyed. Frankly we were as afraid as we were excited. We felt like Jewish Indiana Joneses—we were the real 'Raiders of the Lost Ark'."

Of course that last joke made us all laugh—my *Abba* could always make us laugh. He had seen the Indiana Jones movie only shortly before and started wearing a version of Harrison Ford's famous hat. We thought it fit him quite well.

I must say that though I asked *Abba* often, I still do not know what was in the vault other than the scrolls. According to *Abba*, the team did authenticate the scrolls as documents from the early *Iron Age II* (1000-586 BCE), making them the earliest non-Biblical insight into the workings of the *First Temple* Kingdom of Israel. This was an amazing archaeological and cultural discovery. In Judaism, we know a good deal about how *Torah* was interpreted and religion was practiced from the gathered writings of the sages and rabbis from about the second century BCE on. This, our oral tradition, was passed on faithfully and gathered into the *Mishnah* and later the *Talmud* during the second century and sixth century CE respectively. But up until this great find little was known about the actual practice of the Jewish religion during the early *First Commonwealth* Period, the age of the great kings of our people, David and Solomon. These scrolls reportedly gave us a keyhole look into the workings of the *First Temple* during the reign of King Solomon himself. Stunning!

My father told me that shortly after the event the vault, along with the entire length of the crude tunnel leading back to the vault, was filled in with limestone and tailings from the other tunnels. To this day, the location remains a well-kept secret, one that my father certainly took to his grave.

In the months and years after the find, *Abba* started to tell us wonderful stories, stories of a fictional character, a young and talented *shofar* blower in the service of Solomon's Great Temple. He would tell the stories at bedtime, at family gatherings, at the *Shabbat* table, and of course during the celebrations of the three great annual festivals, Pentecost, Passover, and the *High Holy Days*.

He would urge us to imagine being there— walking alongside of the priests *Jesiah* and *Hevel*, or walking the roads under the tutelage of the Great Prophet Nathan, or walking in the sandals of all of the many other interesting characters, some historical, others figments of *Abba's* colorful imagination. And of course he would emphasize living a spirit of reconciliation and forgiveness as Jews—a very difficult thing to accomplish with what our people have had to endure.

So readers, imagine being there, as a Jew in Jerusalem at the *First Temple* of Solomon— during these important days. Imagine being able to hear the thoughts of the participants. What really happened? What did it feel like to be a Jew during the early *First Commonwealth Period?* These Jews would have not ever imagined the possibility that the very House of the living G_d would ever be destroyed— not just once, but twice since? The question that most captured *Abba's* attention, and came through all of his stories was this, 'What were our people supposed to really feel on those highest of holy days?'

Today, generally speaking, all of these annual *High Holy Day* events happen around the local synagogue and in the dining rooms of individual homes. It must be so because the last Temple was razed to the ground in 70 CE. Known as The Great Disruption, it was another of so many paradigm shifts for us Jews. Questions abound for modern Jews that would never have darkened *Jesiah's* thoughts, the greatest of which, "How can there be atonement for our sins against *G_d* if there is no Temple to bring sacrifices?"

Today, in place of the myriad of bloody sacrifices prescribed by the *Torah*, in place of the prescribed annual gathering as a single people at the Temple of *G_d* in Jerusalem, in place of the experiential *shekinah* glory of *G_d*, we must instead come, as we are, where we are, to the local synagogue. There, in the presence of the *Torah* scrolls, we perform a variety of prescribed *mitzvah*—good works, rituals, and repentances that we hope might gain for us the mercy of the *G_d* who is both near and so very far away. What *Abba* learned from the non-existing scrolls and shared with us is that as beautiful as the *High Holy Day* events are today, they are still only a mere shadow of the same events during *Iron Age II* Israel.

During *Jesiah's* time, the *High Holy Days* were an urgent global event without equal at any other time of the calendar. The events almost exclusively revolved around the Great Temple of Solomon or its immediate vicinity. Within those twenty-two days, vast numbers of specifically prescribed sacrifices were witnessed. Jews and Gentiles gathered from all of the nations to participate and watch. The surrounding countryside was crowded with a sea of *booths* set up by pilgrims from the north, south, east, and west— a multitude of people, all singing the fifteen 'going-up' songs of King David (Psalms 120-134) as they journeyed from their homes, some from very far away, to come as commanded by the *Torah*. There they were met by the professional Temple choirs and musicians, huge public gatherings, feasts and dances, and of course, the important ceremony of the goat for *Azazel*. *Sukkoth* was such a huge international event, that it was merely called, 'The Party,' even by Gentiles.

For the *Jesiah* of my *Abba's* bedtime stories, <u>nothing</u> seemed more important to the events of the holy month of *Tishri* than the experiential reality of G_d dwelling with Israel. I wonder, as my *Abba* did, if since that time our people have always poignantly felt the absence, a nagging murmur of discontent residing deep in our souls. Perhaps even now, though we have been restored to the land again, could it be that in a very critical way we remain in a spiritual exile? Not that *G_d's* Spirit would ever leave His people totally abandoned, but it seems that tragically, His particular *shekinah* glory, His *Kabod,* has indeed remained distant to us. I imagine the difference in the manner a father and his small son walk down a long road together. In one case, the son walks behind his father; the father always looks forward. In the other case, the son is in the intimate embrace of his father. These are both similar and yet very different. Perhaps we Jews have spent much time walking behind our Father.

This is perhaps my father's greatest legacy to the people that he loved. I do not in any way seek to diminish all of his archaeological efforts, his myriad of lectures, the many publications that gained him such public renown and awards. But he himself would say that nothing that he ever did was more potentially valuable to the future of Judaism than these stories.

This is my goal. Archaeologists are not done with their tasks until their findings are analyzed, catalogued, and at last published and made public. How can non-existent scrolls be catalogued and published? For *Abba,* this is to be accomplished by the publishing of the stories that he faithfully shared with family and close friends over the last years of his life. Now at least a portion of his greatest find, the one that 'didn't happen', is being published for the entire world to enjoy— and in particular for the enjoyment of our people, Israel. As much as *Abba* loved us, he loved Israel all the more and continually longed for her peace.

The Shofar Blower
This is the story of *Jesiah,* the *shofar* blower. He is a fictional character. As far as I know there was no *Jesiah,* or maybe many *Jesiahs.* But the Judaism that this *Jesiah* bears witness to is quite real and quite authentic, but so very distant from the Judaism that

17

we so proudly embrace today. I make no apologies for our Jewishness, the Judaism that I was raised in. I have inherited a wonderful people and religion. My roots are ancient and worthy. I am proud of who I am, but not inflexible in things that are meant to be flexible.

Now, without delay, come with me to the *High Holy Days* at the Great Temple of King Solomon, almost 3000 years ago. The Temple is always busy— the priests, the *kohanim* scurrying around, people yelling orders, worshippers bringing bleating disruptive animals to be inspected and sacrificed. It seems that there is always noise, always a wide variety of smells, always stuff happening. Thousands of people are employed to keep the temple going throughout the day and night. The Temple is alive, and it is the institutional heart of the people of G_d.

The Judaism of *Jesiah's* day is significantly different from the post-exilic Judaism of Ezra and Nehemiah, and for that matter, the turbulent Judaism of Jesus of Nazareth's day. This was long before the Jews had any concept that this very same Temple would ever be destroyed. Today, of course, there is no Temple at all in the heart of Judaism. Today, there exists a vast spiritual hole in the soul of G_d's people. We heroically rally to fill the hole with wonderful ritual and event, yet the empty space remains.

But in *Jesiah's* day, the Temple is the powerful experiential source of calling, identity and narrative for the Jewish people. This is true all year round— but the volume of scurrying, odors, sounds and frenetic activity dramatically increases three times a year during the three holy convocations commanded to Moses by G_d Himself, each corresponding with harvests in the land. Of the three, by far the most important and most well attended festival is the Great Feast of *Tabernacles*, also called *Booths*—or *Sukkoth*. This is so vast an event that even pagans, non-Jews who came just referred to it as 'The Party.'

For the Jew, nothing is more important and more critical than the event that immediately precedes "The Party". Of course I am speaking of *Yom Kippur*, also referred to as the Great *Day of Purgation*, or the *Day of Atonement*. At this time, all the crimes, corporate and individual, against G_d, man, and creation are not only paid for, but the vile residue, the sin-stench, is washed off of the people of G_d and completely rid from the Temple. This single event annually sets us free. Here the Jew can by faith access a powerful alien forgiveness—the entire community can experience a real reconciliation.

Jesiah is a young man; one of those people relatively unnoticed in a crowd. He is of average height, average build, more or less brownish hair and eyes. His only real notable physical trait would be a slight male-patterned baldness exacerbated by the way that he ties back his frizzy hair that is just now beginning to rob him of his youthful appearance. Looking at him, you would not call him young or old. *Jesiah* doesn't stick out.

He has gone to his small dark cubicle on the Temple grounds primarily to escape the oppressive Judean sun and to put his *shofar* back in its protective chamber. *Jesiah* is a *shofar* blower. His father was a *shofar* blower, and his father before him. Such is the calling of firstborns, a calling that *Jesiah* freely and enthusiastically embraced. He showed a proclivity towards music early on, mastering many instruments. But he was always emotionally and spiritually moved by the *shofar*, arguably the most important musical instrument of Judaism. It was the *shofar* that blew under Joshua's orders when the walls of Jericho fell like mere tent canvas. But most importantly, and this is not missed by *Jesiah*, it was the sound of a *shofar* that beckoned redeemed Israel to the foot of *Mt. Sinai* to meet with *Adonai*, to at last be in his very presence, the official *'lipne Elohim'* (See Glossary). The ancient phrase *'lipne Elohim'* literally means, 'in front of G_d's nose', but as an idiom it refers to experientially being right in front of the Living G_d. This is what drives *Jesiah* ultimately: to experience the presence of G_d personally again and again.

Maybe the best way to describe *Jesiah* is 'serious'. He, even as a young child, took things seriously. He was one of those annoying children that asked questions all the time. While other kids were out playing silly games with their friends, *Jesiah* would be trying to figure out the very secrets of the universe. He has been told many

19

times that he gets this from his father. His father could have been a great scholar teacher if he had not been called by <u>his</u> father to be a *shofar* player. This was not a regret or a disappointment to him. He too, like his son, felt the importance, the honor, of being a keeper of the *shofar*.

Jesiah still remembers his father's calm, deep, inquisitive voice. It has been years since his father died and was gathered to his people. When *Jesiah* thinks about him, his memories are clouded but warm. His father had not seen this Temple, this great Temple of Solomon. He had served during the transition period and had actually witnessed the amazing day when King David had transported the Ark of the Lord (see *Ark of the Covenant* in Glossary) into Jerusalem. But no doubt he would have loved this new home of *G_d*, here on the same mountain that Father Abraham offered his only son Isaac, only steps from where *Jesiah* now sits in his tiny sparse apartment adjacent to the Great Temple courtyard. Here *Jesiah* sits in his shared, nine by nine, unadorned cell, at his small poorly lit wooden table seriously (as usual) writing down his thoughts and observations for all posterity.

It is the first of the Jewish month of *Tishri*; the fall festival activities have begun only minutes before with the blowing of *Jesiah's shofar*. Israel has been called to the holiest of convocations to be '*lipne Elohim*' in the very presence of *G_d* Himself.

Shalom,

Dr. Ehud Baruch Jr.
1st of *Tishri*, 5769

20

1

The *Shofar* Blower

Jesiah's Journal Entry #1
First of *Tishri*, Before Evening Prayers
It is still hot!

I am very pleased today with my performance and, of course, the sound of my *shofar*. It is the First of *Tishri*, and this is the day when the Temple *shofars* must blow loud and clear to officially announce the annual celebration of *Adonai*'s ascension to His throne over all Creation as the Righteous King in order to judge the entire world. This is the day when justice and reconciliation is announced to all of the nations. G_d Himself is our immediate audience, and so a great deal of preparation and practice goes into this annual moment.

Today was a glorious time. Those around me commented how they had become quite aware of the presence of G_d and His favor upon us. Others spoke of an inner burning. Amen. I hope so. Some were suggesting that this could be another celebration to remember, as it was two years ago when G_d's powerful presence came into the Temple.

As I write this, I am placing my *shofar* back in its protective white linen wrappings. It is a beautiful *shofar*, and I am not the only one who has said so. I must say that I am quite sure that the other *kohanim* are somewhat envious, in a professional manner of course, nothing unseemly.

The late summer air is dry and hot this year, unseasonably so. The current drought in the land is a major subject of conversation and worry on the streets of the city and even here in the Temple. Water rations are in place; more are expected. Special care must be taken for the instruments, for they can dry out very quickly in this stultifying heat. *Shofars* must be kept from becoming too dry and brittle or they will crack.

I remember, for it was not long ago, my final rite of passage in my long musician internship: to prepare my own *shofar*. I looked long and hard for the appropriate ram's horn, smooth and curved, no less than three handbreadths, but had been frustrated at every shop and every farm. After what seemed like weeks of searching, but was more likely days, I was beginning to wonder if G_d perhaps had another calling for me. What good is a *shofar* blower without a *shofar*? Behold the impatience of young men. But to my surprise, G_d had just been waiting to provide for me in a very strange, miraculous way.

It turned out that one of the Temple's many stables had caught on fire when a servant's oil lamp broke, tragically burning all of the animals to death. Among the deceased livestock was a virile, spotless champion ram that had been vowed to G_d by a fellow *kohen* to be a burnt offering to G_d, an *'olah* (burnt offering; see Glossary). The other priests did not miss the irony here; but of course it was not humorous at all. This dedicated ram was indeed an *'olah*, just before its time.

It was around this time that I had one of those fleeting thoughts, you know how that happens sometimes, just a brief moment when I wondered to myself how a *kohen* was able to afford such a grand ram for an *'olah;* certainly not a *kohen* in my pay grade. *Selah!*

But praise be to G_d, *Qayin*, the owner of the ram, heard about my plight and would not rest until I assented to take the charred ram's horn for my *shofar*. *Qayin* was a short stubby man, with a balding pate and a noticeably protruding girth; his face was dominated by his intense bushy eyes and full black beard noticeably graying with age and spreading aimlessly, untrimmed over his bull-like torso. His stubborn intensity and passion, both of which could ignite very quickly, were unmatched among the *Levites*. He was a force and had quickly risen through the ranks of his tribe to a position of significant influence and leadership. *Qayin's* reputation was unspotted, a man who feared G_d and obeyed the commandments, and for that reason he was greatly honored to be chosen as the assistant to the *High Kohen* on the upcoming *Day of Atonement*. This expressed the *kohanim's* great confidence in *Qayin*; well placed in his case.

On the day of the fire, *Qayin* was immensely distraught, and repeatedly urged me to take the only thing left from his burned 'vowed-to-G_d' ram that was salvageable, a single perfectly shaped horn, indelibly blackened by the flames, dark as coal from *Senir*. I think that he felt that it was only right to give the horn to the Lord's service somehow, since the ram was, after all, a dedicated *'olah*. He said, "Maybe G_d will see my generosity and be merciful to me, for now my ram is once again an *'olah*."

At first I refused the gift. I did not want to benefit from another man's tragedy, and he was clearly devastated by the loss. That did not sit well with me. But *Qayin*, who is known for his ability as a persuader, would not take 'no' for an answer. It seemed extremely important to the bull-headed *Qayin*. In fact it seemed quite an urgent matter that I accept this gift from him as to the Lord's service.

I chuckle even now at the stubborn expression on *Qayin's* face as he virtually demanded that I take the charred horn from him. I recall, not too long ago, the sight of a small bedouin lad, no more than 100 pounds wet, if that. I remember him clearly, helplessly tugging with all of his weight on the reins of an incalcitrant old mule that would not budge off of his fat hairy rump. The ass had the same expression that *Qayin* had that day. I will say no more. The point is that it was foolish of me to keep resisting. Who could resist the desires of *Qayin*? Not I. It was an awkward moment, but I acquiesced to *Qayin's* insistent urgings.

But there was a second, equally troubling matter. As I examined the horn more closely, I was not even sure if it was at all redeemable. It was so charred from the unfortunate fire. But after a few long days of careful cleaning, cutting and polishing, I put it to my mouth, pursed my lips, and the sound that rolled out of the perfectly spiraled horn was brilliant, as rich and full as its color was dark. Amazing sound. I have never heard anything like it. I named my black horn, *Yir'eh* (See Glossary)—a pun of course, for the Lord has both 'provided'— and He sees things that are in things that are not.

Today, we the *shofar* blowers rang out the majestic *'tekiah'* in unison, a short but generous bass note followed by a long rich single note for nine beats interspersed with the lively warning voice, then the *'teruah'*, a rapid succession of nine high notes and the most difficult of all of the *shofar* sounds. We practice this a great deal—for it must be perfect. It is written in the *Fourth Scroll*:

"In the seventh month, on the first day of the month, you shall observe a sacred occasion: you shall not work at your occupations. You shall observe it as a day when the horn is sounded."

It is all in the technique of the tongue. *Yir'eh* has never sounded more rich and distinctive. No wonder *G_d* was pleased with us. *Yir'eh* is itself a redeemed instrument that today ushered in the drama of Israel's annual redemption. It makes me laugh. *Hinneh*! *G_d* has provided the ram. He has *yir'eh'd Yir'eh*—He has provided provision.

2

The *Kabod* of the Lord

Then Moses said to him, "If your Presence does not go with us, do not send us up from here. (Exodus 33:15 NIV)

Jesiah's Journal Entry #2:
First of *Tishri*- After Morning Contemplation

As I write this, I am reminded that it was only two years ago when the Holy disruption took place. I was not far from this very spot when G_d's awesome glory, His *kabod* wonderfully and violently came upon this very Temple.

The time passes so quickly. I remember clearly being so shaken that I almost dropped *Yir'eh*. It remains an embarrassment to me, though no one seems to have seen my clumsiness. Perhaps it <u>was</u> seen and yet any witness has been merciful enough to refrain from mentioning it publicly.

The great King Solomon had finished praying a glorious dedication of the Temple to G_d when, I will write what I saw without embellishment, a white reverberating fire came down from heaven and totally consumed all of the burnt offerings, all of the other sacrifices; every single one of them was gone. But that is not all that happened. The most unbelievable thing occurred that had not happened since the time of the Prophet Moses himself. The very *kabod* of G_d physically (I cannot think of a different word for it was palpably present to us) filled the Temple. I, still today, truly lack the words to describe exactly what I felt. I was overwhelmed with a deep unimaginable awe, fear and fullness, peace and joy, all at the same time. I cannot describe it further, for it was not 'like' anything else I have ever been aware of.

Without thinking I just bowed. It was the only appropriate thing to do; my face on the ground pointed toward the Holy. I have heard that this was not just me. Everyone did this in perfect unison. We were compelled to do so. I do not know how many minutes passed or who started the chanting. Perhaps it was the *High Kohen* or maybe King Solomon himself. But imagine the thrill of thousands of stunned and frightened people equally touched as they helplessly and wonderfully were captured in the personal presence of G_d, the *lipne Elohim*. We began to sing in unison, "He is good; His love endures forever...He is good; His love endures forever... He is good; His love endures forever." The images and emotions of that moment are permanently impressed on my soul. I will never forget how the multitude of voices intertwined and magnified *lipne Elohim*. It was as if a gigantic wave crashed over us, rolled back and forth, washing us in an ecstatic glory. We were forever changed.

We had heard, of course, from the *Sacred Scrolls* how the Lord filled the *Wilderness Tabernacle* in the very same way[i]. It is in the *Torah* scrolls and the subject of much investigation by students and sages alike. Of course that was hundreds of years ago now; there are no living witnesses. But now we shared their experience of the Eternal; a touch, no doubt of what Adam and Eve felt. "He is good and his love endures forever."

In the aftermath of that moment, each of us present that day knew that it was now to be our calling as personal witnesses to speak of this to all subsequent generations. It must never be forgotten, for certainly, never again will G_d need to fill another Temple. This is His Eternal *Holy Place* on Earth. *Amen.*

3

The Coronation of the Lord

Author's Notes: *Now as we look over the narrow shoulders of Jesiah, he is shirtless, unashamedly paired down to his undergarments in order to keep as cool as possible. Periodically he wipes the sweat droplets that have beaded up on his broad forehead. He is sitting again in his stark miniscule apartment, with sparse lighting and very little privacy, to write to subsequent generations of Israel as an eyewitness of the grand Coronation of G_d event (see Glossary). His observations as an inquisitive scholarly observer of culture and religion, and keen insights as a musician, would no doubt have made his late father very, very proud.*

Jesiah's Journal Entry # 3–
The *Coronation of G_d Memorial*

Still so very hot in the city! Very little breeze to speak of.

I love the *shofar* and everything about it. I love the regal, penetrating, reverent sound that it makes as I blow the '*teru'ah*'. There is something holy, something awesome, in its resonating undulations. I am not criticizing other instruments at all here. I say this not just because my duties are related to the *shofar*. I can speak to this topic with some authority. I am proud to say that it is my life's calling. The musically ignorant may not know that the sound of the *shofar* is quite specific. There is another trumpet sound on other occasions. But on this day the *teru'ah* splits the silence announcing that the Great King has arrived, but not just any King. *Adonai, Ha-Melekh ha-Kadosh* of all the cosmos is now here. It is here on the First of *Tishri* annually by a holy convocation, that *Adonai* is celebrated in all of Israel as the King of all of the Celestials. At the *shofar* sound we remember, and become recalibrated to the truth that G_d alone is the unassailable Creator King. He is the ideal judge ruler, the King who alone is over all, and who has ordained and empowered order in the cosmos. Amen.

To the uninitiated, today's songs and liturgy with their reported conflict between metaphorical primordial entities may appear almost pagan. May G_d forbid! It is true that other cultures around us also have an annual enthronement celebration for their gods. I am told that in the great lands to the East, they annually celebrate the victory of Marduk over the primeval flood Tiamat. Interestingly, it would seem that much of the poetry in our hymns borrows freely from these pagan concepts and myths. One of our teachers has said that *Adonai* readily incarnates the crude husks of the world; meaning that *Adonai* freely uses the languages, imagery and other cultural icons to communicate His plan for us. I wonder in my heart if this is partly done so that the ignorant nations can hear the familiar among the unfamiliar and that they too may come to know *Adonai*.

The pagans of the *Hatti* land, Egypt, and the great nations of the East all speak of their high gods entering into a violent struggle with *Chaos* before the beginning of the world. In their fantastic mythology, *Chaos* is most often imagined as a huge turbulent sea, pounding waves and floods. *Chaos* is barely defeated but remains an ongoing threat to not only creation itself, but to the victor gods. It is my understanding that the annual enthronement festivals for their deities are not only a memorial of the primordial victory of order over *Chaos*, but also to magically give their gods the power

28

somehow, from the offerings and chanting, to be victorious in their ongoing struggles. Unlike Israel, the pagans do not speak of their deities as continually residing on an unassailable throne. Their gods must struggle annually with the powerful entities that make up *Chaos* in hopes of defeating them.

This is not so for us. Today was not a day when we empowered *G_d* for His struggles. That would be absurd. He is not in any real struggle whatsoever. *G_d* is already the Cosmic King and cannot be defeated, seriously challenged, or in any way dismissed by the other so-called gods. The Scrolls tell us that *G_d* created the entire cosmos with a single utterance to ultimately reflect order. Our forefathers in Egypt were wrongly taught that the cosmos order, which the Egyptians called *Ma'at*, was above the gods. But the *Torah* tells us that this is in no way true. *G_d* is far above all *Chaos*, and above order for that matter. He, unhindered and unchallenged, speaks into the *Chaos* and boundaries of order are spoken into existence— created where there were none before. His proclamation of order is perfect and thus will be, <u>must be</u>, completed in the days to come. His Kingdom is moving now to conquer all residual *Chaos*.

Today, we, the people of *G_d*, gathered to remember, to re-experience, that *G_d* is now and is always on His unmovable throne. Not unchallenged, mind you, for perhaps in the eternal realm there are would-be accusers and usurpers, though I cannot speak of such things from my position. But the challengers, whoever or whatever they may be, amount to absolutely no serious threat to the singular throne of *G_d*.

We came today to the Temple to sing Coronation Hymns to *Adonai*. It was a solemn time, joyful and awesome. The schools of *kohanim*, dressed in holy garb, bright white linen robes, lined up on either side of the immense, gleaming white stairs of the larger court and sang with all of their might, sometimes in perfect unison and at other times *antiphonally*. The celebration opened with the *shofar* blast, *"terua'ah!"* followed by another, and yet another. Today, when I blew *Yir'eh*, I imagined that I felt all creation shake

29

and *Chaos* wobble at its knees. But of course that is only the speculations of a foolish servant.

Then the *High Kohen* choir on the right hand side of the steps of the Great Court erupted into great voice:

Adonai is become King
Adonai is robed in Majesty
And has girded Himself with might
Indeed, the world is made ordered
It will never be shaken.[ii]

Then the mixed *kohanim* choir on the left hand side of the stairs turned toward the *Holy Place*, the place where *G_d* dwells, and responded with equal forthrightness, speaking directly to *G_d* on our behalf,

Your throne is established from of old
You are from everlasting.[iii]

They repeated this celebratory verse until it had seeped into all the nooks and crannies of the Temple, cleansing, setting the stage for all that was to come. The Director then nodded to a smaller group of elder singers, who stepped out of the general choir and began to sing in lower melodic tones as if telling a story. They spoke in heightened poetic language using imagery to describe the aggregate challenges to the dominion of *Adonai*. The song imagined all the forces that foolishly attempt to usurp *Adonai* as a flood of chaotic waters; like a massive *wadi* flood, the waves pound three times upon the legs of the throne…

The floods have lifted up, Adonai
The floods have lifted up their raging
The floods have lifted up their pounding.[iv]

The same choir then sang this chorus twice more and then bowed, humbly disappearing like a gentle undertow into the sea of singers. Then the first great congregation exploded in a breaker crescendo of joyful response, as the song imagined *Adonai* and His throne totally unmoved by the triplet of hoary usurpers.

Greater than the rantings of the forces of Chaos
Greater than the raging waves of the sea
Adonai is on His high throne.[v]

This was immediately followed by the entire congregation worshipping the unassailable King of the Eternals. I admit that I too joined in at this point, though quietly, for singing is not my calling or, if I were to be very honest, my gifting. We corporately turned to face the *Holy Place* and bowed our heads to the ground. This was a solemn stunning moment, for we addressed the G_d-Who-is-with-Israel; the G_d-who-hears-us.

Your statutes are unmovable and trustworthy,
Holiness rightly adorns Your house
Lord, for the length of days.[vi]

It is as if the participants in this oratory became part of the giant waves themselves, rising and falling, only to rise again.

But in the end, the aggregate waves bowed to proclaim *Adonai* as Lord. Our Lord, unlike the fragile gods of the nations is so glorious and firmly on His Judgment seat on high, that He merely looks down to casually notice the violent floods and great waters of *Chaos*; all entities, persons and nations who would dare to challenge Him and His verdicts.

Today, the First of *Tishri*, we celebrated the enthronement of *Adonai* over all the celestials. We celebrated the enthronement as if G_d had stepped down for a time and is only now returning. But in truth, He never stepped down; never has He bowed to any challenging power. Yet, on this day, we re-experienced the re-enthronement as if new. We re-experienced the event as if it was on this very day that He first rose to establish order. Today, the Great King sat on His throne officially to judge all the world. Though it is from of old, the enthronement of the Lord is always celebrated as on 'this day'!

For me, the pinnacle of the day was the sixth of the celebratory songs. This is the one in which *Yir'eh* proclaimed its place in *Adonai*'s plans. There was an extended silence after the

31

previous solemn psalm.[vii]   The Choirs made way for the instruments: the harps lined up on the bottom stairs, next the trumpets on the next five or six stairs going toward the *Holy Place* and finally the *shofars*. We proudly (but yet humbly of course) took our place on the top steps and waited patiently for our time.

The harps began with only a single rich note, in full unison. The main choir on the left hand side of the stairs (as I stood looking over them) began in earnest but not too loud at this point.

> *Sing to Adonai a new song*
> *For He has done unimaginable things*
> *It is His right hand and His holy arm that have made liberation on His own behalf…*[viii]

All of the events of the day required a new song from Israel, a fresh record and proclamation of events past. The subject of the song was *Adonai* alone. In this we were clear, as Abraham was before us. It is the work of the Lord that salvation and redemption were given to us. We, His people, are not innately special among the nations. No. But we are wonderful in glory because of *Adonai's* election and purposing. He alone must provide the lamb, as always. No one of Israel may boast of more than that. The other choir (on my right and below) sang back in response.

> *The Lord has made His salvation known*
> *And revealed to the eyes of the goyim His righteousness.*
> *He has remembered His covenant promises*
> *And His faithfulness to the house of Israel;*
> *All the ends of the earth have seen the salvation of our G_d.*[ix]

The psalm reminded us this day again, that our mission, entrusted to Abraham, Moses, David and now us as *G_d's* chosen, is to further the propagation of the redemption of His Kingdom throughout <u>all</u> the goyim (the nations). It is a huge unbelievable charge that is entrusted to Israel; clearly a mystery beyond our capacity and comprehension. The psalm invited all who have come to enter the newly redeemed wave of former *Chaos*.

Musically, the psalm reached its crescendo as the waves reached their pinnacle height. The command was for all voices from all of the earth, all nations, to shout in acclamation and acknowledgement that He alone is G_d; it is He who has made us. *Amen?*

At this, the crowd that has gathered was invited to participate. They had been patiently waiting for this moment of the day. Now they enthusiastically cried out in praises. The choirmaster repeated this chorus until the crowd was hoarse:

Shout in acclamation to the Lord
All the earth
Break forth in sound
Make a joyful cry
Sing praises...[x]

Then the strings began to play, even over the din their voices could be heard:

Sing praises to the Lord
With the lyre
With the lyre and melodic voice...[xi]

But, if I must say so, everyone was still waiting, holding back just a little for the pinnacle of the movement. At last, into the din, the trumpets and the *shofar* together began to boldly blow "tari—ooo" "tari-oooooo!" "tari-ooooooooooo!"

With trumpets and the sound of the shofar
Hari'ooo...[xii]

The choir continued watching the Director closely now as the cacophonic sounds of the people and instruments were bouncing off the stonewalls and odd shaped corners of the Great Structure!

In the official presence of the King Adonai
Let the sea roar and everything that fills it
The world and all who dwell in her
Let the floods clap their hands together and
Let the mountains cry out in joy

THE JESIAH SCROLLS

In the official audience of Adonai
For He comes to judge the earth
He is judging the world in fairness and all people in equity.[xiii]

   Amen, Amen and *Amen.* It seems to me that this was the heart of the day. Not only was *G_d's* throne proven again to be unassailable by any usurping power, but even the very floods themselves were redeemed and came to see, to *yir'eh*. They too groaned for *Chaos* to be rid from them; they too longed for *G_d's* verdicts. The very nature of the *lipne Elohim* required a necessary resolution of all injustices, reparations, and cleansing from corruption and sin for all peoples. There is no other court in any land anywhere that would dare to make such a glorious claim. *Selah.*

4

The Royal Wedding Procession

Author's Note: *Why do people often pick the most inappropriate day to have their wedding? As we catch up to Jesiah and his journaling, there are only a few days until Jerusalem will swell five to ten times its normal population, not to mention the thousands of animals, large and small that will clog the highways and tight streets, along with the noise and intense smell that follow such a congestion. Rosh Hashanah and Yom Kippur are upon Israel, and Sukkoth, The Party is only a week beyond that.*

But there is even more at play here in Jerusalem this day. This was a holy season, then and today, for reverent introspection, for fasting and praying—not at all appropriate for a marriage, particularly such a controversial one.

So who would even think to plan such a wedding, any wedding in this holiest of times? A King, of course. Things haven't changed so much in that arena. People of power can still pretty much do what they want; they often overlook the effect of personal decisions on regular people.

Today, Jesiah was joined by one of his closest friends, Hevel, one of the sons of Asaph. The Biblical Asaph was a prominent Levite Priest and one of the leaders of David's choir. The so-called 'sons of Asaph' were probably his

35

disciples who served in the Temple as singers, poets and musicians. Some were described as prophets.

Hevel is relatively young, but was fast-tracked due to his impressive wisdom in many matters. Perhaps 'prophetic' is a good description of Hevel.

Culturally, wedding processions occurred well after midnight. The dark streets were brightly lit up by a variety of torches and makeshift firebrands. Some care would be taken to avoid the fire spreading to the surrounding wooden shop fronts, but it was always dangerous. This evening there was a dry desert coolness in the night air, a very welcomed respite from the scorching heat of midday. Jesiah had to run back to his cell for his overcoat, the one that his mother had given him years before when he entered the priesthood. He wrapped it around himself tightly and ran to catch up to the other young priests.

It was well after the third watch when Jesiah finally made it back to his cell. To the chagrin of his very weary and noticeably irritated roommate, he lit a couple of oil lamps, untied his scroll, and intentionally went about the business of writing down his observations of the evening; his many thoughts and feelings. It does not take much for young men to dream about their own weddings. Certainly Jesiah's would not be as glorious as Solomon's, but aren't all weddings royal, at least a little bit?

Jesiah's Journal Entry #4 –

It was very late. *Hevel* and I went down to the royal courtyard to watch the arrival of the newest bride of King Solomon, the pagan daughter of the *Pharaoh* of Egypt. It caused no small uproar among the priests. Not only was his marriage to a non-Jew, but also the event was very colored by the timing. Who would initiate a marriage, any marriage between the blowing of the *shofar* and *Yom Kippur*, a time when men, and in particular the King, should have their minds on other things, holier things? It is so very inappropriate.

Hevel is my best friend, certainly one of the more theologically-minded Sons of *Asaph*. A couple of years my junior, he is maybe in his late twenties. *Hevel* is long and thin and walks with a lanky gait. His face is as long as his stride; both his bony jaw and extensive nose draw attention away from his already

36

unimpressive brown eyes. His skin is the skin of youth. Since he is betrothed to be married in a few months, I joked that he could pick up some pointers from King Solomon's wedding. We all got a good laugh out of that. Even the rationalist *Hevel* appreciated the absurd humor and blurted out a sort of chuckle. It is not so easy to get *Hevel* to laugh. He thinks too much— at least that is my opinion.

In typical weddings (non-royal that is) in families of some social weight, there are often two processions. First, there would be the bridal procession to the home of the groom. Usually at night, it was customary for it to be led by flaming torches, singers, musicians and dancers. The bride would be on a grand horse or in an elaborate covered *palanquin* following other animals or servants carrying her trousseau, gifts, and other property. The joyous procession would take its time winding through the city streets on its way to the home of the groom. The groom would not be there, and the party must wait for him to arrive.

It was not until usually after midnight that the groom, with great pomp and fanfare and with all his friends, would begin his procession. Crowds would gather in the streets, balconies and rooftops to see the groom in all his splendor. Cries of "Look, there he is!" and "He is coming, He is coming!" would ring throughout the dark streets. As the entourage approached his house, the bridesmaids would come out to meet him with candles and torches, making straight the way to his house and his waiting-bride.

But for royal weddings, and in particular royal weddings of such international status as this one, there is only one procession. King Solomon, the great King of Israel, would send an immense military entourage to bring his bride-to-be to his royal residence. They would return to Jerusalem, to his palace, in a huge gala event— a citywide celebration. And, since pilgrims were in Jerusalem for the *High Holy Days* anyway, this event was larger than ever recorded for a marriage of an Israelite king. Perhaps that was King Solomon's plan all along. But believe me, the priests are not enamored by this encroachment. Not at all.

Nevertheless, it <u>was</u> grand. Today, camel after camel wound through the narrow streets already clogged with visitors. Each was adorned with ribbons, jewels, and feathers; innumerable trumpets blasting the arrival; oriental dancers in troops and singers galore. I noticed a large retinue of Egyptian musicians skilled on wooden flutes, harps, lutes, drums, and a variety of metallic clappers.

Then came the military escort, impressive by any measure. Seven columns of *Melee infantry*, seven men across shoulder to shoulder and seven men deep, equipped with spears, battle axes and other weapons such as daggers at their side. The spears were as tall as the men, their highly polished broad-leafed copper blades caught the reflections of the surrounding torches and flashed like lightning bolts in the night. Their battle-axes hung at their sides, large and foreboding. Each of the soldiers carried a colorful new shield – about five feet in height and made of leather— it would appear. The colorful decorations shockingly carried crude images of strange Egyptian gods and goddesses. It was a terrible intrusion; particularly now, at this time and in this season.

The soldiers were followed by 100 huge archers, Nubians from the Sudan no doubt, their skins pitch black, a head above even the tallest of Israel. Nubians are reputed to be quite skillful with the bow—even at 60 yards! They were giants to us. The crowd automatically moved back further out of their way.

Colorfully decorated chariots followed them— dozens it seemed, though I stopped counting. Each chariot was manned by two huge soldiers drawn by regal black stallions that pranced ahead of them. These must have been the great men, *Pharaoh*'s own bodyguards, sent to protect his daughter on her marriage journey.

Following them were dozens of Egyptian priests. We recognized them by their unusual dress: only loincloths with a bright white linen kilt, and baldheads. They walked, in bare feet, immediately in front of the princess's *palanquin*.

Oh my, what a *palanquin*! Six broad-chested white stallions drew it. It was box shaped, with four raised corners, hammered gold over every side and corner. It was draped with brightly colored regalia, dyed linen curtains, and huge plumed feathers, ostrich perhaps. On its sides were painted rows and columns of Egyptian hieroglyphs that told stories of great romances of legend and magic incantations to empower fertility and cause many royal offspring. Surrounding the *palanquin* were royal guards, each with a sword at his side and each willing to give his own life to protect the princess. It was difficult to look directly at the *palanquin* from the side we were on as it flashed the reflected fires from the torches in all directions. Oh, how it appeared to dance in the light. The red curtains were drawn, but no doubt the princess was inside and enjoying the enormity of the honor of this event. Or maybe, I wonder, if she was beginning to worry what her life might now be like, the queen of a people who were not her own.

The princess' maids followed the *palanquin*. They were beautiful women with their facial features highly magnified by the stark make-up they used. Each wore a typical Egyptian wig, with the blackest of black shoulder length hair and straight cut bangs. Egyptians shave all of their hair off as children (to prevent lice we are told) and so the women, poor and rich alike commonly wear wigs. They were wearing bright white linen full-length dresses that were held up by the thinnest, most delicate white shoulder straps. I must say that their collective beauty took my breath away, but there was one young maid who particularly caught my eye. She was not as dark as the others, virtually milky white; her eyes were green and bright. I wondered what province, what people she hailed from. It was her eyes that I remember still— green like grass, but brighter, almost glowing. Perhaps it was the make-up, but I don't think that I have ever seen a more beautiful woman.

Each of the women, including my favorite, wore a treasure of jewelry: gold, silver, and precious stones. No copper or bronze here, not in this parade; these were royal servants and courtiers.

The last part of the procession was made up of carts and carts of Egyptian animals and produce, clearly in preparation for a great feast. Huge well-fed sheep, a dozen cows, even more goats, crates of ducks and geese, racks of abundant dried fish; donkeys laden with a plethora of vegetables and herbs. I could see marrows, beans, onions, lentils, leeks, radishes, garlic and lettuces, melons, dates, figs and expensive pomegranates. I wondered at the contrast between the splendor and extravagance of this event and our drought-ravaged local economy. We have no Nile River to keep the land fertile. We must depend upon Yahweh. For His own purposes, Yahweh has withheld the rains for these recent years. No one outside King Solomon's court will eat as well this entire year as those at his wedding on this day. I did catch my stomach growling at the sight of this bounty. Fortunately it's complaints just could not be heard over the din.

After the procession ended, *Hevel* and I wound our way up the many staircases to the Temple grounds. His wedding would be a few months hence, but much more modest of course. Priestly weddings are indeed wonderful affairs; truly sights to behold. The Temple courts are adorned with flowers and wreaths, flaming torches, and no shortage of musicians and singers. However, they usually cannot afford any processions, much less royal ones replete with golden carriages, Nubian archers, and wig-clad beauties. On the meager salaries given to us, it takes great discipline and fortune to even save up a bridal price, much less the price for the actual wedding itself. *Hevel* was one of the most disciplined men I have known.

He had been saving up for a long while before he even met his bride-to-be. I am pretty sure that his family helped him. His uncle's family, I think, was not in the priesthood and owned some profitable property north of Bethel. They give *Hevel* a healthy stipend in addition to his priestly salary. G_d is very gracious. Amen?

Other priests, and to be honest me as well, had eyes on his betrothed even before *Hevel* did, but it was not meant to be. She is a young maid in the Temple kitchen. *Tamarah* is her name. She is almost perfect in shape and feature. Her hair is pitch black and wavy, her stature is strong, her figure curved. When she laughs, her eyes leap out at you. She is the favorite with all whom she serves, though, no doubt, this makes her the object of jealousy to other women there.

40

I do not begrudge my friend's fortune at all. I was in no position to approach *Tamarah's* family. I certainly did not then, nor do I now, have the ability to support a wife, even one as productive and capable as *Tamarah*. I would love to be a husband and father someday, but I cannot count on help from my family since both of my parents passed away, and I have no rich uncle that I know of. So I must put aside a bridal price on my own; a very daunting task I am finding.

I still remember *Hevel* getting his nerve up to ask *Tamarah's* gruff father for his blessing for their union. *Hevel* is a thinker, a philosopher musician, not a negotiator. He left his cell fully bathed and sharply dressed in his best priestly garb. He was so nervous that he almost tripped going out the door. It took a very long time we thought. When he at last returned to the cell, he was covered with sweat and white as a sheet. He tried to tell us what happened, but couldn't remember any details. Even though he had practiced what he would say over and over, for days, he had no idea what he actually said to *Tamarah's* father. The entire event was just a blur in his head. All he remembered was that her father did at last give him his blessing and that a bridal price was agreed upon. We tried to be gracious to *Hevel* as we listened to his strained story, but all we could do was laugh. At last, someone broke out wine for a toast. *Hevel's* head was still spinning; he just sat there dazed and broadly smiled.

I must say that the betrothal was life-changing for *Hevel*. I have seen this before with others. His confidence seemed to grow daily. He was already quite a capable priest before this, but now, lets just say that he blossomed like a field flower on the Plains of Sharon after the winter rains. Praise G_d that *Hevel* has found a bride in Israel. May G_d richly bless him with many young *Hevels* and *Tamarahs*.

I have been attracted to many girls, and I am pretty sure that a couple of them responded to my flirtatious advances. Among my fellow unmarried priests I would classify myself as somewhat handsome. As a youth I remember local girls laughing at my massive frizzy hair that always looked like an explosion had occurred on my head. This was from my mother's side of the family, as my father could count his remaining hairs on one hand. But now, that same hair tied back with leather ribbons is considered quite a boon and attractive to women, or so I have been told.

There are perhaps some marriageable priests who are taller (I get my height deficit from my mother's side as well) or have more striking features, but I am clearly among the more marriageable I think. A bride could do worse, no doubt. *Shofar* players command great respect in Israel. Good *shofar* players are assured employment for as long as they desire, and I am a very good *shofar* player. I will someday be able to provide for a family, maybe even a large family. I have five brothers and four sisters, and many fond memories. I know that I will be married at the right time. *G_d* will be gracious to me and give me a seed.

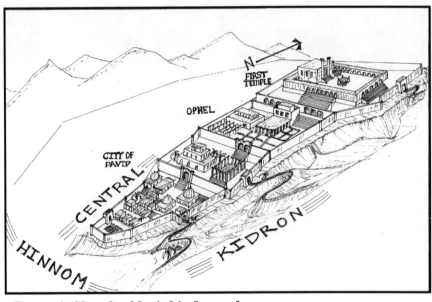

Figure 1- Sketch of Jesiah's Jerusalem

5

Oh Jerusalem

Jerusalem built up, a city knit together, to which tribes would make pilgrimage,
the tribes of the LORD, — as was enjoined upon Israel —
to praise the name of the LORD.
Ps 122:3-4 (JPS)

Jesiah's Journal Entry #5

I spent the morning out of the Temple campus doing errands. It gave me a chance to do my own sightseeing. I pretended that I was a pilgrim, maybe a farmer from the *Negev* who was coming to Jerusalem for the first time to these holy days. I was given eyes to see as he would.

Today Jerusalem is a city strategically situated on what appears to be a single stepped oblong ridge. But I remember when I was a child, the ridge was a series of three separate hills, or better plateaus, running roughly north to south with the deep *Kidron Valley* shouldering the east, the Valley of *Hinnom* on the south and the shallower *Central Valley* on its West. The southernmost hill has long been the foundation bedrock for King David's magnificent fortified city, formerly *Jebus*— the site of a glorious ancient history. It is a low, rather narrow ridge really, only 150 yards wide in some parts, and surprisingly one of the lowest hills in the area. What made it the necessary place for the actual fortification? The Spring of *Gihon*, the only water source in the entire region, is actually in the *Kidron Valley*, unfortunately slightly outside the original eastern walls of King David's city. Our engineers and architects expanded the fortification to enclose the spring so that the city is virtually impervious to an attacking army and normally fresh water is readily available.

Not too long ago there was a narrow shallower saddle immediately to the north of King David's fortification, which then rose to a smaller plateau some 35 yards above David's City. This is popularly referred to as the *Ophel*.

Immediately to the north of the *Ophel* was another larger oblong north-south ridge about twenty yards higher than the *Ophel*. This is where I stand this very day, the present Temple *Mount*, but it was also the home of the threshing floor of *Araunah*, where King David came face to face with *G_d's* judgment for his crimes of adultery and murder.

In the last number of years, contractors have successfully filled in the two saddles in the north-south line of the ridge, making it for all practical purposes a single ridge which rises from the Pool of *Siloam* and the confluence of the three main valleys at its southern tip, rising some 60 yards over two abrupt terraces as one moves northward.

Travelers from the southern *Negev* regions would first see the Royal City as they ascended the ridge of hills just to the south, across the *Hinnom Valley*. That would give them a most magnificent view of the entire complex of rising terraces.

It struck me as a marvelous thing for visitors to the city during this Holy time to experience the upward movement as one enters in the south and climbs the multiple extravagant stairs and porches to arrive at the Great Temple, even as the smoke of the *'olahs* go up *lipne Elohim*. It is truly a moving experience. Supplicants, who would be *lipne Elohim*, must always go up. Amen.

As the traveler heads northward across the *Hinnom Valley*, they will most likely enter the fortified walls of David's City through the well-traveled *Fountain Gate* near the place where the *Hinnom* and *Kidron Valleys* meet. Others might rather come in from the southwest across the *Central Valley* into David's City through the *Valley Gate*. But either way, as the visitor looks northward toward the *Temple Mount*, they are keenly aware that they have a difficult and long upward journey still to go— a 50 to 60 yard rise in a very short geographical distance. My favorite path takes me along the luxuriously terraced King's Gardens, though at this time of year there is little to see there really. In the spring it is a stunning place. I can only imagine what the rest looks like, the section that is closed off for royal use only.

Once the visitors have climbed stair after stair and made their way through all of the new construction on the former *Ophel*, they at last enter the glorious porch of the King Solomon's Royal Palace complex. Immediately before them is the House of the Forest of Lebanon, aptly named due to the 45 massive cedar columns which rise over 50 feet high. For travelers who come from rural districts, this is always a sight that takes their breath away. The porch itself is 50 feet wide and 82 feet long. To access the porch, the stairs rapidly rise some 30 feet and are bounded by palm trees, giant ornate vases, and vendors selling their wares to hapless tourists every day except the Sabbath of course.

Once inside the Palace complex itself, there is other equally impressive architecture. There is the second porch of pillars just off to the east, fronted by steep stairs. There is the actual throne room of the King to the northwest, along with the extended royal residence itself. I have never been in either of these buildings. Currently a great deal of construction is underway to expand the residence to house the King's growing number of wives. At midday, the sun's rays flash from the copious copper plating throughout the complex. It is said that the wealth of Israel and of course the young King Solomon has been largely built on the abundant copper mines of Edom[xiv] and the massive smelting operations on the *Wadi Arabah* both conquered by King David.

The reflection of the sun's rays off the walls, columns and cupolas can be positively blinding.

It is only when visitors pass the sprawling palatial complex that they finally can see before them the massive ornately adorned steps that lead into the actual Temple itself. This gate is one of the most holy of course, and is surrounded by huge impressive copper plated columns, with artwork and foliage prescribed by *G_d* Himself. Remember, to be *lipne Elohim*, it requires a going up. *G_d* truly does dwell in the heights.

6

What are We to Feel This Day?

***Jesiah's* Journal Entry #6-**
Before midday cessation of labors

I have just returned to my Temple quarters from a very interesting conversation with *Hevel*. He was without peer today, in pinnacle prophetic form. The hot sun is reaching its zenith in the sky and so I have retreated to the coolness of my stone cell for respite and to write in my journal. I feel a wispy, somewhat cooler breeze blowing through the windows. It is quite welcomed.

For a number of days now, I wanted to ask *Hevel* what he thought this larger Holy season was all about. My question to him was, "What are we to really feel in our souls as we enter into these holy days?" Everyone knows what we are to do, of course. It is all highly scripted and practiced to perfection. We are professionals. But what should we be experiencing?

I am a naturally curious person and so I look forward to any opportunity to dialogue about *G_d* and His Temple. *Hevel* was also in the Temple, two years ago, when *G_d's kabod* entered. He is one who clearly has taken the time to ponder the event and he is always willing and ready to give his opinions. But honestly, I had no idea that he had so much to say about the matter. It was as if I had unplugged a deep gushing fountain. He responded almost immediately as if the matter was well rehearsed in his mind. I have done my best to recall clearly what *Hevel* said, though certainly I have left some of his comments out. He summarized his thoughts by saying that the entire season, from the first to the 22nd of *Tishri*, is a "celestial invitation from the pursuing G_d to His alienated people to come into His presence in order to be cleansed by G_d Himself so that they can once again truly experience the deep covenantal intimacy of the Great Feast of *Sukkoth*."

Wow! That is a very heady thought. I confess that I had never considered the season in that way, that the benefit of these weeks is primarily for mankind— for us— as much or more so than for G_d. I was curious to know how he came to such a radical conclusion. Though his comments, as expected from *Hevel*, were extensive and heady, this is, I hope, a faithful rendition of what he said:

"It is obvious, of course, that the history of our people, the people of the Creator G_d *Adonai*, has been marked with... no... slashed with crises and catastrophes. Some good and positive; others devastating, but each calling for dramatic adjustments that necessarily have reoriented our lives. In each, G_d has been faithful, beyond our imaginations and comprehensions. Sadly also, of course, we have fallen short of covenant."

"Technically speaking, the first great crisis was a positive one, at least for our people Israel. Of course I am speaking about the Exodus. The *Torah* tells us that we were set free, not by any human power, but only by G_d alone. We were a beat-up people— and no doubt had begun to believe that we were a trash people— worthy of nothing but serving others, objects strictly for the pleasure of others, a people of victims. But in a mere moment, we were not only set free, witnessing such a devastation laid upon the Egyptians, the greatest military and economic power of the day, but equally shocking, we were reminded that we were, in truth a great people under G_d."

"It is said that so many of us in the bowels of Egypt had tragically forsaken *Adonai*. We turned away and began to look to other gods, the gods of Egypt: *Ma'at, Isis,* and *Ra*. It is humanly understandable (not justified or right, mind you). From our perspectives as slaves there appeared to be no *Adonai* in the land of Egypt. We had no scribes, no *kohanim*, no King, no prophet. We could only see what we could see. There was no reason, humanly speaking, for us to see *Adonai*."

"But *Adonai* pursued us with a purpose in mind. He sent the savior Moses, who led us from the darkness of slavery into the official presence, the *lipne Elohim,* and so proclaimed by G_d Himself as worthy guests of honor. Do you see? This juxtaposition would have been awkward, very uncomfortable and even unimaginable to our forefathers. We had not even cleaned the dust of Egypt, and the smell of slavery and idolatry off of us, when we were invited into the Holy presence of the same G_d who crushed unclean and rebellious Egypt."

"Listen, because this is very pertinent to your question. What were our people feeling? You and I would <u>never</u> come before the Lord apart from a sanctifying bath or a sacrifice appropriate for the time and purpose. But our forefathers, fresh out of Egypt, had no such preparation. They didn't have time to become ritually clean, or to bring sacrifices, or to do any appropriate exercises of penance. Imagine. There was no altar even to make *qorban* offerings. They felt like smelly garbage in the presence of Glory!"

"For our forefathers, there was no Holy place to clean and prepare for G_d. We stumbled to the *Holy Place*, in this case the base of the mighty granite behemoth Mt. *Sinai*, that G_d prepared for Himself and which He Himself declared clean. Of course, in hindsight, we see that we did not need to be afraid. It was after all G_d Himself who had called us to audience, with arguably minimal personal consecration, for the most part we came as we were, with our soiled, abused and empty hands. Technically speaking we were there at His invitation so there was no need for any *qorban* offering. But still, can you put yourself in their sandals?"

51

"So there we were. We stood, or rather, we bowed, in the valley of the great mountain *Sinai* and quaked as the trees quaked under His thundering voice. We just knew we were lost. We felt afraid, ashamed and naked before *G_d*."

"But, of course, our fears were unfounded. Our expected destruction was not to be. *Adonai* is wholly other, not at all like *Pharaoh*. In hindsight we can wonder about much of what the events meant, but clearly this can be said. *Adonai* did not bring us out of Egypt and into the desert to kill us, or punish us for generational unfaithfulness."

A rush of questions fumbled in my head, but only one rushed to my lips. I was struck, and maybe a bit offended by something that he said, "*Hevel*, how were our forefathers unfaithful?" Was going to Egypt in the first place 'unfaithful'? It seemed to me to be an obvious choice for our forefathers in the middle of an extended famine to leave the land, for survival reasons alone. Didn't our people in Egypt under the great Patriarch Joseph multiply?

My friend paused to think about his next words. Perhaps it was only a dramatic pause for emphasis, for that is the art of rhetoric. He smiled and rubbed his sparse beard, not yet full enough to be attractive as a man's beard should be. But still the gesture did indeed make him seem older and wiser. His eyes glimmered with a youthful spark of light and a broad toothy smile erupted on his face. He jumped up on a nearby column base, swung the folds of his priestly white garments around him and struck a pose, the pose of a lawyer, or perhaps a rhetorician, and certainly better suited for a much larger and more distinguished audience. But nevertheless, he was certainly enjoying himself. For a moment, he was a world-class logician, overflowing with gravitas. He was *Hevel* the Great Sage who was answering a question of the ages.

"How were our forbearers unfaithful, you ask? Point number one. Is it not written that the children of Jacob did not involve *Adonai* in their decision to go to Egypt? They left the land of promise to venture down to Egypt and Joseph's care, without an audience with the *G_d* of covenant! No doubt, in human wisdom, it would seem to have been a wise thing to do. But we understand, do we not, that the beginning of wisdom is the fear of the Lord? You might argue that they acted in wisdom that was spawned from the fear of hunger, the fear of destruction. You might retort that they were just using the wisdom that *G_d* gave mankind, and expects them to exercise; that they were exercising good old-fashioned *binah* (discernment- see Glossary) to choose between two paths. But, there are two kinds of *binah*. There is human *binah* on the one hand; and then there is *binah* that exclusively comes from *G_d*. The latter is given to those who specifically request it from *G_d* in humble faith."

My young teacher was quite insightful. His words were truth. We have heard of course how King Solomon himself went to *G_d* as a youth to ask specifically for the gift of *binah*. It is said that he knew he needed it so much that he offered a *qorban* of 1000 sacrifices to *G_d* before *G_d* answered him: "Ask for whatever you want me to give you." The King, a mere teen at the time, asked *G_d* for discernment, for the ability to rule over *G_d's* people as the ideal King. *G_d* was so pleased with the King's heart and desire that He gave Him both heavenly wisdom and discernment.

The surprising display of rhetoric continued as *Hevel* leapt off the column foundation and briskly walked in long, lanky strides around the hall, continuing to make his grand arguments to his audience of one.

"Look around you, listen to the many proverbs of the King. You would agree, would you not, that *G_d's* discernment and wisdom is much greater than our own. Only *G_d* sees the past as well as the future. Only *G_d* in His perfect wisdom and discernment can rightly judge all trials. My suggestion to you is that the children of Jacob in this act of omission were unknowingly guilty of hubris before *G_d*, gross self-sufficiency. Arguably, this is unbelief, plain and simple."

Hevel could tell that I was a bit confused and so he redirected his logic to another narrative that I was familiar with from the *Sacred Scrolls*.

"My second point: Is it not also written that the sons of Jacob stayed in the land long after, in fact, generations after the drought

53

was over? Amen? By the time of the Exodus no doubt they had become more Egyptian than Hebrew. It is written that they cried out in their misery, but it does <u>not</u> record that they cried out to *Adonai*. A sad, tragic gap in the narrative to be sure."

Then, with clear lawyer tonality, *Hevel* put forth that this was indeed covenantal unfaithfulness. "Wouldn't you agree?," he asked looking straight into my eyes—leaning close enough to me that I could see again how paltry his beard was. *Hevel* paused, walked a little way down the Temple corridor and continued.

"I would hope that I have convinced you of our people's implicit rebellion, perhaps not *high handed*, but complicit in sin nonetheless. No matter what our forefather's sin or possible defense might have been, they were <u>not</u> brought out to *Sinai* and an audience before *G_d's* face to be slaughtered. They were brought into his presence to be <u>honored</u> as chief among all the people— a people to be raised up as His *segullah*, his special treasure, to be part of a restated and reshaped political/social alliance with *Adonai;* and they, we, were to become again His intimate bride of great promise. These were the very same contractual promises made by *G_d* to Abraham, the promises made to Noah, the promises made to Adam and Eve. *G_d* once again was making a straight path back for us into our unique covenant relationship."

He began to wave his hands in the air to emphasize his points as he made them now in tight series.

"So what then did they feel? Can you imagine the huge *Sinai* crisis in our people's hearts and souls? Our fathers and mothers were slaves of slaves of slaves. In many ways, no doubt, they were more Egyptian than Abrahamic, perhaps followers of many gods and idols. Ah yes, does that shock you my friend? Is it not imaginable that many of them grew angry and hard-hearted by their gross inhuman mistreatment for so many years? After being defecated on by so many for so long, it is natural to become a skeptic of *G_d*, or even perhaps an unbeliever, eh? Amen? But all of Israel, all of us were gathered together at the base of the Great Mountain, *lipne Elohim*, and invited to be guests of honor at the

54

banquet table of the Creator of the Universe. This would have been beyond the comprehensions of our people."

"What a shock to realize that we were not refuse as we had been told for so long; we long buried any aspiration or hope. Relegated, resolved to just survive another day, another week, and now to come to this moment? Were we really, this whole time, people of promise? Instead of being burned at His feet, the elders, former slave captains, were invited to eat with *Adonai*—guests of honor. No one knew how to respond to such a radical and stark turn of events."

Hevel sat down on the top of a staircase that led up to the living quarters. The activity in the hall was increasing as the time for the *Kohanim* choir, a highlight of the day, was almost upon us. He lowered his gaze. It seemed to mark the seriousness of what he was about to say.

"This was not just a philosophical shift in a cold theology. Not a change of ownership from one *Ba'al* to another; a new set of guidelines and rules to observe or be punished severely. This was wildly different!! Do not miss this or the events of the upcoming *Day of Purgation* will be meaningless to you. We were reminded at the foot of the fearful *Sinai* amid the thunder and lightning that we were no ordinary people, or certainly not slaves as we had been told for years. We were still the people of the promises. The stories that the slaves had told their children slaves were real; at least most of them."

Hevel grinned broadly at this last light-hearted quip. He was truly an entertainer.

"There really was a covenant G_d, *Adonai*, who had committed himself to us years before, generations before. He had not forgotten us in our weaknesses and in our foolishnesses, remaining in Egypt instead of returning to the land of the Patriarchs. G_d remained *Adonai* to us, faithful. What had we been thinking? Why were so many years and lives wasted?"

"Unbelievably, G_d's first act was to actually offer the blessing of hospitality to Moses and the Elders. We were despised slaves only days before. Only weeks before we had cleaned up after the

55

banquets of Egypt. But now, here we were, guests of honor at the banquet table of *G_d*? Incredible!"

"Fellowship meals were not uncommon in those days. The educated knew the meaning of such ceremonies. *Adonai*, the Great Creator, King of the Cosmos, was bending down to eternally align Himself with the smallest of people; a marginalized, weak and beat-up people. Yes, even an unfaithful people. Cleary it was glory covenanted with garbage. This was not punishment, but instead He was publicly making our names great. He spoke to us as a Great *Suzerain* King would to an honored faithful vassal King. "I am your *G_d*, and you are my son." This was an act of great honor, something of the like that only *Pharaoh* could have boasted of in Egypt. But *Adonai* had proven that He was beyond *Ma'at*, *Ra* and *Isis*. He stood over all as King and Judge."

"Of all the peoples on the earth, He is pleased to uniquely be our King and Lord. He spoke of us as His sons and daughters, or even more provocatively, as His bride. In a matter of days, we went from being a lonely alienated people with no hope, to being an embraced people with promise of greatness."

"But…," I interrupted his extensive argument to address what appeared to be a problem of logic. "*Hevel*, I am following your logic to this point. Our forefathers at the base of *Sinai* had bestowed upon them by *G_d*, more honor and mercy than they knew existed previously. But what I cannot explain is why then, they— and we— then turned to idols. It seems to me that such kindness would lead to the worship of *G_d*." I can see now as I write in my journal that *Hevel*, the logician of logicians had set his careful trap, which I was more than pleased to step into.

"Ah *Jesiah*, it is good to see that your head is not just used as a source of wind for your *shofar*. There is great glory to you. You are correct in your concern. It is true that people of substance and glory are moved and attracted by such honor. But not slaves, and certainly not generational slaves birthed from the loins of other slaves. Follow me here, for this is the kernel of my answer to your question about what we are to feel. There is no way our forefathers were able to comprehend the magnitude or to be in any way comfortable in the wash of the covenantal graces of such a vast G_d. Even the newest of *kohanim* know the rest of the story. Moses alone went into the frightening thunder and lightning to hear from *Adonai*. Forty days, forty nights."

Being long after the midday meal, he finally paused, no doubt recognizing his stomach's pangs of hunger. *Hevel* reached into the fold of his robe and took out a loaf of bread, clearly a loaf that had time to harden. He tore off one of the edges, breadcrumbs bursting into the air, and put a piece in his mouth. It was clearly harder than bread should naturally be and so it took some time and obvious struggle for his mouth to defeat it. But the larger portion of the hard tack he now used as a prop, a pointer that he pointed directly at my face. The rhetoric moved forward now with no less energy than before.

"Where was I?... Oh yes. Moses was gone for so long, there was reason to wonder, to speculate, to let our imaginations, our slave hearts wander—to run amuck. This is much too good to be true. We knew perfectly well that we were not worthy of all this honor; this new name. We were not ritually clean, morally and ethically no better than Egyptians if the truth were known. We were <u>not</u> the people that *Adonai* thought that we were. Can you imagine the long days and nights, the rumbling of internal and no doubt external speculations?"

"We must recognize that slaves are survivors. There is not anything we would not do to <u>not</u> make a mistake. Mistakes have consequences; usually to be publicly ridiculed or whipped by our masters. So we strategized to avoid making a mistake.

Jesiah, follow our forbearer's logic here. Certainly, no god smiles on laziness in his or her presence. So G_d must be waiting, watching to see if we are worthy. The only model we had were the rituals that we had watched at a distance in Egypt. It was an honor to the Egyptian gods to make a model of them and to bow to them. It was an honor to perform ritual dances and to sing songs. Certainly we need to be the people that he thinks that we are. We slaves know survival. This is what you do. You do something. So we conspired to take matters into our own hands and do something—do anything."

"I have come to see that even today each of us is <u>still</u> very much afflicted with that very same slave mentality—and feelings of course. It is the dark backwash of the very sin that afflicted our mother Eve and our father Adam immediately after the very first catastrophe. After taking of the unnamed fruit (by the way without running to G_d for discernment) all *Chaos* broke loose. For the first time, they felt stark fear *lipne Elohim.* It was not 'fearful-awe' of a good *G_d*, not spectacular breathtaking wonder, rather pure unadulterated fright. This fright, by its nature, didn't draw them toward *G_d*, but pushed them away. They hid. Please make a mental note of this, for it is the essential aspect of the *Day of Atonement* to redeem and purge men of this seminal fright."

"But there was no place to hide at the base of *Sinai,* so the fear had to play out another way: foolishness. Oh yes, you looked shocked? Did you not know that foolishness is much related to fear?"

"That was not all that our forefathers felt. They knew the shame of their father Adam and mother Eve— that sense of nakedness and helplessness before *G_d*. Until covered, these feelings only furthered their the sense of separation. Until covered, no man can feel comfortable in *G_d's* audience, in His embrace. Thin pitiful leaves provide little respite."

"And you can be sure that there were not sufficient leaves at the arid barren base of *Sinai* for all of our people. So we had to act out quickly. As slaves do <u>so</u> creatively, we took matters into our own hands. We made ourselves an idol; no doubt the intention was to create a favorable portrayal of *Adonai*. Certainly we thought He would be pleased. But more importantly, we hoped that He might be swayed to favor us on the basis of our service, on the behalf of our strivings on His behalf. After all, we were slaves. This is the way the world works for slaves. You do well; you are rewarded or at least minimally not whipped. If you do <u>not</u> do well, keep the gods and masters happy, keep them smiling toward you, you <u>will</u> feel the bite of leather on your back."

"This is important for us to grasp during *Tishri*. We still <u>feel</u> very naked and uncomfortable as called-out people. We still <u>feel</u> suspicious of honor, very suspicious of honor from superiors. We would have far more preferred rigorous costly sacrifices where we could earn *G_d's* favor, or even the beatings of harsh justice. We would do *qorban*. Isn't it the wise and discerning thing to do?"

I nodded automatically. Amen, it sounded reasonable to me.

"But you know the story. We came to see that *Adonai* was not at all like the other gods with which we were familiar. These actions at the root of the mountain weren't the fruit of wise and discerning thought; rather they were the foolish actions of slaves, perhaps well-meaning, but nevertheless actions of ignorant slaves burdened with fear and guilt, unable to feel honored, unable to feel clean just because we are in the presence of the one who makes clean, unable to feel welcomed."

"Our fathers then, had no capacity to experientially enter into the glory bestowed upon us that day. We couldn't really 'believe', not in the highest sense. Our post-Edenic slave-faith was a far cry from the higher faith of Abraham, who truly believed *G_d*, so much so that he was boldly willing to sacrifice his son Isaac. Our fathers and mothers at *Sinai* couldn't relate to that. They couldn't comprehend such good news yet, that *G_d* <u>always</u> provides His own sacrifice on the behalf of His elect. The latter need only helplessly receive with their empty soiled hands. It is *Adonai* that pursues and unilaterally redeems unworthy victims. As it is written in the *Second Scroll*,

"The Lord! The Lord! A G_d compassionate and gracious, slow to anger, abounding in kindness and faithfulness, extending kindness to the thousandth generation, forgiving iniquity, transgression, and sin; yet He does not remit all punishment."[xv]

"This is <u>whose</u> we are. This is our ongoing story and ongoing struggle to fathom. This is the story behind the liturgical pinnacle of our year, the days between the first and twenty-second of *Tishri*.

59

It is an age-old story, the golden thread that proceeds through the *Sacred Scrolls*. When *G_d* says, 'I am your *G_d* and you are my people', He speaks of a time not only in the future, but also of time present, for all who by faith humbly will go up and enter His presence. We still initially come these days as slaves. We initially feeling the same feelings of shame and fear again."

"On these days, *G_d* continues the process of restoring mankind to Eden. *Adonai* desires a single bride, persons who can feel loved, feel grateful, feel adored; a single people which He Himself is preparing, empowering, setting free, wooing, releasing from debts, and making 'clean'. *G_d* must do this Himself, for we, His people are so quickly straying and pursuing other gods; gods who feel safe for slaves"

"Why does He do this? He desires that this Bride would be truly free, at long last willing and able to finally stop thinking and acting like slaves and start acting more like a great Queen in His embrace!"

"But, alas, we are naturally the children of our fathers and mothers: wayward and foolish. We regularly wander and stray from His presence, no doubt partly out of foolishness and unbelief, partly out of spiritual adultery (the other gods are quite attractive to garbage— very well packaged for slaves), and partly out of fear and guilt. It is particularly the latter that drives the drama of this Holy season."

Now as before, my *kohen* friend took on the demeanor of a great lawyer beginning to make his final summation.

"What roles do fear, shame, and guilt play in the drama of these days? Simply put, the latter drama is designed primarily..."

At this he raised his hand skyward and points up, perfectly staging his comments. His enthusiasm still makes me laugh to myself quietly.

"... first and foremost to enflame, expose, and eventually dispel the former. Let me explain. The further we are experientially from *G_d*, that is, the more that we have embraced the world, the more successful we are, the more compromises that we make, the more we get used to this fallen existence, the less guilt and shame and fear that we feel <u>on the surface</u>. This is just a common human phenomenon. Our relative and the first murderer *Qayin* (Cain) left the mess that he caused near the gate of Eden and went <u>down</u> away from the presence of the pursuing compassionate G_d. We should be able to quickly relate to him with even a little honesty and self-awareness. As a consequence of his crime, *Qayin* would naturally feel a swirling aggregate of guilt, pride, fear, confusion, the desire to escape, to run, to blame someone, and to cover up. He did what we would probably do in his place. He ran and built the first city. Cities have walls of course. Most of the walls are designed to provide security and order for the residents. But for *Qayin*, the walls were no doubt constructed to keep the pursuing G_d away. To men of wisdom and discernment today, it sounds so foolish, but we do it all the time in so many ways."

"The further that we run away from *lipne Elohim*, to turn our eyes, to use our reason to doubt *G_d's* existence or His goodness, frankly, the better we feel, at least on the surface; if by that we mean no longer do we feel the ever-present piercing stab of guilt, shame and fear. Away from Him, we do not need to look into His eyes. We don't need to explain our failures again. We don't need to explain why our very core identity is driven to such self-destructive folly. We don't need to fear seeing His anger, or worse, His gross disappointment again. Are you following my logic up to now?"

I nodded in approval.

"This running away is what we do for eleven months out of the year. Do you realize that the very moment that we leave the joy of *Sukkoth* to return to our usual *'amal* (burdensome toil), we begin to forget G_d, and of course then, by cause and effect we forget who we are <u>in</u> G_d. We turn to any means to fill the void. Almost every step down from the Temple to our homes is a step emotionally away from our source of life and identity. It isn't long before, like our father *Qayin*, we are hiding behind similar walls and eating at his stale banquet…"

61

THE JESIAH SCROLLS

I looked directly at his hardtack pointer. He got the joke immediately, and though his cheeks blushed, he never lost composure, pointing the stale loaf right at me.

"...Yes! Our hearts hardening just like my lunch here. But we are slaves from slaves and we have learned to manage."

"So, back again to your question. What are we supposed to feel during these Holy days? *Jesiah*, at a certain level we feel great discomfort, emotional disruption, and an inner turmoil. The closer we come *lipne Elohim*, the more experientially uncomfortable all of us should feel. With every step up to His presence, we will feel dirtier, increasingly unprepared, more and more ashamed and unclean. We will naturally feel the need to avoid *G_d*'s penetrating gaze, the celestial whip on our backs. Excuses, self-justifications, *qorban* offerings, illustrious prayers for mercy, quick acts of generosity and *mitzvah* to hopefully add something meritorious to our year. For those who are spiritually aware; a visceral fear bubbles up from the deep recesses of our hearts. It is always there, slaves are always slaves, and victims are always victims. But the closer we get to the Temple, the more aware of we become of the fear that has powerfully motivated us the rest of the year. In fact, if *G_d* hadn't graciously commanded our audience year after year, we would not come. Every step upward toward *G_d's* presence ignites within us the nascent fear, shame and guilt that have been our *Ba'al* all year. Most of us are blissfully unaware of our ongoing enslavement."

"What is it that we feel as we come up to the Temple? Freshly exposed fear, nakedness, failure, and shame. The upward journey is very uncomfortable to all of us. This is *G_d*'s purpose. It is the covenantal love of *G_d* at *Yom Kippur* that alone has the power to strip us, for a moment, of our fear, to purge us of innate guilt and shame. It has the capability to at last set us free from our many *ba'als*. This is His heart: to annually clean us from this inner lie. So my dear brother, for just one moment at the end of *Yom Kippur*, the participants, no matter who we are or what horrible crimes we may have committed, sins of omission or commission, we actually become the pure children of *G_d* again. We become human for just a moment. We regain the humanity of Adam and Eve. It is *G_d* who unilaterally knows our proclivity and has orchestrated this event to purge us of our 'slaveness', wash us from all of the residue and filth of our crimes and unbelief—for at *Sukkoth* we <u>will</u> actually <u>feel</u> a desire to dance in *G_d's* presence. This is the whole point of His judgment at *Yom Kippur*."

Hevel emphasized 'will' brilliantly and then began to dance around the corridor. *Hevel* is an insightful scholar and teacher, but a very poor dancer. Lanky and awkward, less like a gazelle and more like a camel, in fact, a stiff camel with a big toothy grin. I laughed and couldn't resist joining him in his pathetic dance. Together we sang and danced until one older *kohen* barked out a complaint from a nearby cell. We laughed all the more.

"*Jesiah*, here we come as redeemed slaves to the foot of the Mountain of *G_d*, and we are purged of all of the lies within us once again. It is here during the *High Holy Days*— *lipne Elohim*— that we are changed, reborn— if you will, married again to *G_d* as if we were untapped virginal wells. Here we become truly human again. Here we have become once again, a single people under one *G_d*. Here we feel like sons of *G_d* again. Here we are made Israel once again. Here we dance as a single people for the first time in 12 months."

Our conversation and dance both ended as each of us had duties to attend to. What could I say? *Hevel's* logic was masterful, surprising perhaps, but beyond debate it seemed to me. I wonder if *G_d* loves us that much. Is *G_d* actually happy with me right now, as I am— not based upon my efforts on His behalf? I realize that in the back of my mind I really do think sometimes that my efforts are necessary for *G_d* to favor me more. I admit that I often do things so that *G_d* will hopefully bless me, give me honors, or at least not punish me. I wonder sometime if *G_d* is withholding a wife from me because I did something wrong or I am not up to standards in some area. Sometimes, I even think that *G_d* loves me more because I am a *shofar* blower. Am I thinking like a pagan slave? Is my devotion and service driven internally by the all too human need to make *G_d* love me as a son? To earn something from Him? Is *Hevel* right, that I am bound by a powerful hidden ever-present pagan-fear deep within me that causes me to wonder if I will make the cut on *Yom Kippur*? Do I feel the need to do things for *G_d* before I could feel like dancing at *Sukkoth*?

I remember poignantly that I felt the dance two years ago when *G_d's shekinah* entered the Temple upon us. Now that I think about it, there was a feeling of wild acceptance and joy *lipne Elohim*. I didn't feel judged or criticized—at all. Instead, I felt an alien glory, honor, identity encompass me— as I was— far more than I deserved— not a bit of shame or guilt. It was wonderfully uncomfortable and glorious at the same time. That's it. I felt free from shame and guilt for a moment in time. I couldn't help but dance. Is this what we are to feel every year? Is this *G_d's* desire for His people? For mankind? For me? Not perfection but freedom? Not a reminder of my failure as a son but rather honor as His elected son? Not an annual reminder of the requirements of servitude as much as gracious call to dance as a result of His cleansing embrace? I would like nothing more than to feel this again. But I suppose that much of my day-to-day religion and piety is nothing more than a slave-like attempt to achieve the unachievable.

I smiled as I watched *Hevel's* tall bouncing camel-strides as he journeyed off to his next appointment, still waving his arm with the makeshift pointer in the air practicing his next oration no doubt. A little ways up he stopped to notice Silas, the old beggar who regular sits near the entrance to the temple complex. Silas claims to be from the royal family, but no one takes his rantings seriously; generally he is mocked or overlooked. But *Hevel* didn't overlook Silas. He went across the court to one of the many flat bread vendors that have sprouted up in Jerusalem for the festival, bought the largest flat bread they had and presented it to 'King' Silas with a deep bow of respect and honor. I have to say that I felt a pang of shame and guilt deep within my gut. I have stopped noticing Silas and the many other street beggars. But I also feel pride and wonder at the pure actions of my best friend *Hevel*. As was true for his namesake long before him, I am confident that God looked with favor upon his offering this day.

THE JESIAH SCROLLS

7

The Tourists

Jesiah's Journal Entry #7

Hevel and I just returned from the marketplace with a small bounty. I love the produce of early autumn. I was concerned, for there were many rumors about the thin harvest this year. Israel has been experiencing a drought for over two years now. The desperately needed winter rains have been paltry at best; in some regions there was no rainfall at all. So, of course, both of the grain harvests of the late spring and early summer (wheat and barley) were very disappointing, quite pitiful really. Bread has become a very expensive item, double what it would cost even a year ago. The grape harvest back in the month of *Tammuz* was also lackluster and the olive yields last month were very disappointing. But today I was able to find beautiful figs in the marketplace, not many mind you, and somewhat expensive and on the small side; but those I found were quite flavorful.

Hevel and I also spent the time studying the many pilgrims who were on their *'aliyah*.

We had just entered a courtyard on one of the lower garden terraces when *Hevel* put his left arm around my shoulder and leaned in to whisper something obviously interesting, and knowing my friend, very insightful. He pointed surreptitiously to a particularly interesting family that had just entered the portico. They weren't from Jerusalem, I would guess, for they lacked the sophistication of dress and demeanor of the typical urban dweller. It seemed obvious to me that they were from a rural area, maybe even a poorer area. But the thing that made it clear to both of us that they were not of Jerusalem is their starry-eyed gazing in every direction trying to take in all of the great sights all at once. These were clearly tourists. *Hevel* noticed something that of course proved one of his many theses.

"Do you want more evidence of what I am saying with regard to people's conflict of feelings in this season? Observe those visitors to Jerusalem, over there under the large balustrade just in front of us, to the left of the gate. Obviously from the sticks, Galileans no doubt, here for the High Holy Day. This is their *'aliyah*, their 'going-up'. Do you see? The old man who is leading the entourage is very dour and serious. But the younger man with him? His eyes are filled with life and dare I say, expectations. The old man is wearing sackcloth like us. But not the young man. He seems ready for *The Party* right now."

"Look around! The *Sacred Scrolls* prescribe only a single day of *innui nefesh*, afflicting our souls. Isn't that right? But did you notice that many of the supplicants do far more than that. Some, like that man over by the gate seem to want to be seen as religiously fasting for the entire time, wearing dark and hairy coarse clothes, and publicly afflicting themselves. Still others walk among the crowds not looking at their path, but piously looking up at the heavens while reciting long legal passages from the *Torah*— creating quite a hazard for the traffic around them. They bump into others who probably— only on these days— stop to toss a couple of coins to the many street beggars. Still others refuse to piss within the walls of the city, as if that bodily function was evil somehow, just on these days. Don't miss my point for judgment. I can definitely relate to them. Slaves need to be accepted for what we do. But G_d is not honored, not pleased with us just because we don't relieve ourselves for 10 days."

"It is our residual 'slaveness', our shame, guilt and fear that has flooded into our souls like cascading waves of chaos that is leading to such rank foolishness, such paganism. Yes, that is the right word here. We treat G_d unaware as if He were more like the gods of the pagans than the G_d of Abraham and Moses. We know, don't we, that G_d is not subject to manipulation or bribe, or affected by any actions that would generally cause a human official to relent, to change their minds. G_d's plan is much larger than that. That is 'slave-thinking'. Remember the foolishness of our fathers at *Sinai*. Granted they waited forty days. But it was foolishness nonetheless with painful consequences."

"This very day, on this day of purging, G_d Himself <u>will</u> graciously, unilaterally purify such as these of the shame, guilt and fear that has enslaved their freedom, and will <u>Himself</u> provide the ram's blood to scrape off their— our many sins. None of their actions, or mine, beyond those required by the *Sacred Scrolls* are efficacious to any degree. G_d has specifically prescribed what is appropriate in the decorum of His courtroom. There are only to be the prescribed offerings, no more and no less. There is only one offering that is prescribed to be a satisfactory atonement, a legal satisfaction for all crimes of all the people. The intentional affliction of our souls to earn anything with G_d is not helpful here *lipne Elohim*. So why does *Torah* prescribe such affliction? Clearly it bears witness of our sorrow and repentance, of our deep desire for redemption and salvation. It reflects certainly a reasonable humble posture which is ready to receive the unilateral gift of G_d."

Once again, my tall friend had to lope off quickly; he was late again for some very important appointment at the Temple courtyard. I also needed to return to the Temple and my duties of course. It is a very busy time. But I indulged myself to watch the lanky disheveled *Hevel* bound up two, sometimes three steps at a time.

THE JESIAH SCROLLS

I dearly miss the pungent penetrating smell of fresh virgin olive oil penetrating the corridors and corners of the marketplace. By this time of year, the jars in shop after shop should be overflowing, spilling over with sweet oil, with the sun's heat creating a powerful aroma that seeps everywhere. It is a wonderful smell. But this year, the jars are closed and carefully watched. No doubt there will be many prayers to the *G_d* who ends droughts this year.

8

The Great Disruption: Am I My Brother's Keeper?

***Jesiah's* Journal Entry #8-**

Today the holy reverence of the Temple's outer court was greatly disturbed by *Qayin*, the same *Qayin* whose ram perished in the unfortunate fire. Now looking back at the fire, I remember wondering what *Qayin* was doing with such a ram of great value. It was a very expensive animal, one that would be a costly offering for those of us on *kohen* salaries. I also remember wondering why he was so forceful that I should take the ram's horn to use for *G_d*. Now even more questions flood my mind. This is a tragic day in Israel.

It was just beyond midday, the hottest time of the day. I had retired to my modest cell on the south side balustrade of the Temple's outer court. Though my cell was one of the smallest, roughly nine by nine feet, my two roommates and I find that due to its location on the row, we enjoy an almost constant cooling breeze through our two thin windows. Both windows have beautifully articulated latticework, highly ornamental and colorful. But the important thing to us in the midday heat is that the window is designed to keep the sun's rays out and the cooler breezes wafting in through the trellis openings. This afternoon, my roommates were out and about in their appointed business. Perhaps I had even nodded off. I am not sure. But I become aware, startled in fact by a great commotion in the court, a loud crying out, along with the confusion and commotion that happens when many urgent sandaled feet are running by. I quickly threw on my robe and ran out of my quarters, bounded down the stone stairs to the Temple's terrace level, rounded the east side of the *Great Altar* only to see my benefactor *Qayin* surrounded by other *kohanim*, on his knees prostrate, head down to the ground, his large shoulders heaving in sobs and moans. Periodically he would raise his head, all of his face twisted in deep inner turmoil, crying out to everyone and no one, *"Ichabod! Ichabod!,"* "Forsaken! Forsaken!"

On any day, guilty supplicants who would be restored to favor with *Adonai*, can bring their sacrifices up the fifteen steep stairs that go up from the palace terrace to the higher Temple terrace. The Temple terrace is surrounded by a massive stone retaining wall that is 400 feet wide and twice as long. Three sides of the retaining wall (north, east and south) are made up of three rows of hewed stones and form a colonnade of sorts along with storage and living quarters for those of us who are involved in the Temple workings. The supplicants can bring their offerings in through one of the three gates, each with three sets of side chambers for any business that needs to take place. Each gate also has an exquisite porch that opens into the large Outer Court of the Temple. In the western center of the Outer Court facing east and raised on another terrace some 16 feet above the Outer Court is the rectangular Inner Court complex measuring some 400 feet by 200 feet. It is surrounded by another colonnade of three rows of pillars. At certain appointed times, the supplicant and their offering must climb up the fifteen stairs into the Inner Court's Great Gate. It is on these very steps that we sang the hymns to G_d's coronation memorial only a few hours ago.

In front of them, the supplicant can see the massive unhewn stone altar of sacrifice and behind it, the Holy Temple itself, with its Great Porch shouldered in between the two almost 60 foot tall columns. They will not enter beyond the altar for that would be arrogant and foolish. Their business with *G_d* is at the *Great Altar*. Only the *kohen* can proceed further up.

On the *First of Tishri*, the *Torah* normally prescribes special offerings to be done exclusively by the *kohanim,* consistent with other New Moon offerings. In the *Fifth Scroll* of Moses we read

"In the seventh month, on the first day of the month, you shall observe a sacred occasion: you shall not work at your occupations. You shall observe it as a day when the horn is sounded. You shall present a burnt offering of pleasing odor to the LORD: one bull of the herd, one ram, and seven yearling lambs, without blemish. The meal offering with them — choice flour with oil mixed in — shall be: three-tenths of a measure for a bull, two-tenths for a ram, and one-tenth for each of the seven lambs. And there shall be one goat for a sin offering, to make expiation in your behalf — in addition to the burnt offering of the new moon with its meal offering and the regular burnt offering with its meal offering, each with its libation as prescribed, offerings by fire of pleasing odor to the LORD."[xvi]

These sacrifices are almost identical to the other New Moons of the year. The presiding *Kohen* will present as an *'olah*: one bull, one ram, seven male lambs with appropriate *Cereal* offerings and lastly a purification offering made of a male goat. *'Olah*s, of course are the most common of offerings. They almost always are performed because the supplicant has committed a sin against *G_d*, or feels like they have offended *G_d* in some fashion unaware and they desire to be back in *G_d's* favor once more. This is *G_d's* heart as well. He remembers the separation that occurred when His first Garden-children reached out illicitly in their unbelief. The separation wasn't *G_d's* desire. He pursued Adam and Eve, but they would have none of it and preferred their own 'coverings' for their shame. The *'olah*s are *G_d's* gracious provision for redemption from sin and its consequences.

There is a mysterious aspect to the *'olah*. Unlike our pagan neighbors, we do not in anyway think that there is something innate in the smell of burning goat hair that bribes *G_d* on our behalf. The *'olah* does not remove sin or change our sinful nature, or relieve us of the immediate consequences of sin. Nevertheless, *G_d* for His own reasons accepts the *'olah* as if it was efficacious. It is as if *G_d's* attitude is reversed by the *'olah* and the Holy Judge now smiles upon a sinner; or at least withholds the judicial wrath that is due.

In some ways, it might be helpful to speak of it as a ransom. There is a human precedent, prescribed by the *Torah* whereby for some crimes, a ransom could be paid to the plaintiff or their family.[xvii] Though this concept is not without its difficulties when applied to our broken relationship with *G_d*, it still offers a useful point of reference. It appears that the merciful *G_d* so desires to be one with us that he accepts an *'olah* as a ransom for the supplicant to escape the penalty that would legally and appropriately be due them.

When a supplicant comes to the altar with an *'olah*, normally they lean upon its head with their right hand and publicly confess their crime (if it is known), or sing a psalm, or pray contritely to *G_d* Himself. We understand that the High Judge mystically sees the sins and consequences of sin of the supplicant as legally transferring to the animal. Or if you prefer, *G_d* chooses to allow the animal to take the individual's place in the courtroom *lipne Elohim* and to take the verdict upon itself and die as a legal substitute for the supplicant. This is the essence of *G_d's* justice with mercy. It is fully just, for no crime is ever overlooked or treated lightly. It is fully mercy in that an 'other' in an act of *tsedaqah*, that is righteousness, takes the verdict upon themselves. Our Great Prophet Moses proclaims that this is done so that the Lord may then accept the supplicant without any hesitancy at all. Once again the universe is ordered. There is *shalom*.

Once the words have been said, the supplicant slaughters the animal in the traditionally prescribed manner. The *kohen* catches the drained blood and splashes it on the base of the Great Altar. The head and the fat are now taken by the *kohen* and placed on the Altar. After the supplicant has washed off the excrement from the other parts of the sacrifice in one of the portable lavers near the altar, the *kohen* burns everything remaining on the altar with the exception of the skin that is taken outside the Temple grounds. Through this costly process, the supplicant is now assured of being restored to the favor of *Adonai*.

But today, it wasn't just any supplicant. No, this was the same highly respected *Qayin* who had just recently been chosen to assist the *High Kohen* at *Yom Kippur*. We were not emotionally prepared for this. But there before us was *Qayin* bent down over his offering, and a pitiful offering it was— I will say more in a moment— in the very shadow of the *Great Altar* that he was so familiar with. His shoulders moved in spasmodic motions, sometimes weaving to one side, then to another, or at times violently heaving up and down. He was in pain, obviously filled with remorse, distraught to the very edge of what a man can take. All he would say for the longest of time was "Forsaken! Forsaken!"

His weary hands, body, and even face were covered with dark crimson blood of the picayune lamb whose lifeless body lay limp alongside him; its life gushed out of the fresh gape in its formerly dappled grey-white throat. It took me a short time to see that the woefully inadequate lamb was actually meant to be *Qayin's 'olah*. I would think that such a pitiful specimen would normally be refused. It was not even close to the level of offerings that people would dare to bring. The sight of this heightened the already palpable shame in the air.

Qayin knows all of this, surely. He was a man who once feared G_d and walked in righteous ways. He was always superior in the fulfillment of all of his duties; some said that he set the standard for humble obedience to the prescriptions. But now we see clearly that *Qayin* was not as righteous as was previously assumed. As *Qayin* laid his right hand on the head of this diminutive animal, and leaned all of the weight of his shame upon its head, the corruption of his heart puked out of his mouth as he confessed in great specifics how his life had unraveled before him, so quickly, so easily.

Now my dealings with *Qayin* over *Yir'eh* made more sense to me. I can see now, that *Qayin* had planned on bribing *G_d* with a champion expensive ram. I think of *Hevel's* observations earlier. What folly! Certainly *Qayin* knows better? Or was he so shallow that he needed to save pride among the *kohanim*. "Look how truly humble *Qayin* is, that he would spend all of his inheritance on a single offering—all for *G_d*."

But *G_d* clearly would have none of such a foolish strategy. What was to be an extravagant public *'olah* became a very private shame. The ram was indeed a burnt offering, but not on the *Great Altar*, not public, no laying on of hands by anyone. This explains *Qayin's* great urgency for me to take the ram's horn. It was a last ditch effort to buy *G_d's* favor indirectly? How quickly our hearts are turned away.

All that was left for *Qayin* was this. He must now let go of any clinging to his former reputation, before us, and most importantly before *G_d*. I still see him there, humiliated before his peers, deeply busted, brought low and exposed laying over a very poor offering. There was now nothing for him to lean his hands on at the altar, that is, other than *G_d's* great lavishing mercy. That is all. *Adonai* is certainly bringing *Qayin* low.

It was here in the Temple court, with the flame of the altar crackling just above him, *Qayin*, long beyond the days of such youthful desires, his face lined by age and beard grizzled with grays and whites confessed before his peers and fathers of the fateful day on which he gazed at a betrothed woman with pure lust in his heart; like King David did with *Bathsheba*. He was so obsessed with physically having her that he followed her day after day, spending more time longing for her, even while he was performing his priestly duties and even in his times of prayer.

The latter admission was too much for *Qayin*. His knees folded under him and he lay prostrate in the blood spilled out on the hard limestone floor. He said, "Even as I mouthed prayers *lipne Elohim*, I only thought coarsely of her." He could say no more for long moments. He just moaned and swayed his body as if in internal agony. "I have brought great unwashable pollution into the Temple Court!" He was inconsolable.

This was a deep shock to me. I know *Qayin's* wife. I have dined at their table on a number of occasions. She is a glorious lady cut out of the heroic cloth of Ruth herself, attractive in an older maternal manner. She prided herself on fulfilling the duties of a wife. She was the picture of faithfulness to *Qayin* and their eight children (though his oldest two twin girls would hardly be called 'children' anymore. In fact, I wonder in my heart that they are probably closer to the age of the woman in question?).

Arguably, the years have not been necessarily so kind to her perhaps, but nevertheless it is correct to say that she has retained much of her youthful spirit and joy. She was the daughter of one of the leading men in the closest entourage of the *High Kohen,* a man who like *Qayin*, feared G_d and walked in righteousness. I was told that *Qayin* had earlier confessed his crimes to him. Raging waves of *Chaos* were beginning to roll through the formerly ordered foundations of his extended family even now.

It is strange how the mind works. It was at that very moment that I became keenly aware of the smells at the altar on that very hot afternoon, standing in a crowd under the glare of the sun. The smell of blood was pungent and it seemed to me 'warm', if warm could be a smell. It was intertwined with the rank smell of feces and the sweet odor released when the Arabic gum resin frankincense burned along with the binding in the flour of the *Cereal Offerings*. I was first taken aback, even sickened by the overwhelming power of the stench, but as the lighter aromas wafted into my nose, there was something dynamic in the air that day: life, death. Maybe, I thought in my heart perhaps that this is the smell of justice.

The weary *Qayin* continued his confession as he leaned over the lamb. He confessed that his crime was not in ignorance. He had been fully aware that the woman in question was betrothed to another *kohen*, but it didn't matter. He was captured in his heart's desire, enslaved. *Qayin* had been driven to madness by lust and with the great forcefulness of his personality wooed the younger, emotionally immature woman and convinced her to lay with him in the field; even on one occasion while her betrothed was fulfilling his own priestly service during one of the Spring full-moon celebrations. While the unsuspecting kohen was ministering *lipne Elohim* faithfully and righteously, *Qayin* was bedding his betrothed.

Who can resist the desires of *Qayin*, indeed? I am not a trained lawyer of Israel, but whether or not this was consensual, this still seems to me to be a *high handed* crime. It was certainly a pre-mediated crime of lust that brought destruction into all families involved; and it was perpetrated by a well-respected *kohen*.

To make matters even worse, if they could get worse, the woman in question is now with child—his of course, their child of unfaithfulness. Two families destroyed, a young couple's hopes and dreams shattered by one selfish destructive act by a previously faithful husband, father and *kohen* and a previously chaste betrothed virgin. As of today, *Qayin* had not yet personally confessed to the betrothed groom. He was not sure what he could say. More cries aloud, more wave-like swaying, more bitter self-condemnation, no hope.

The officiating *kohen* was a seasoned veteran of sacrifices. He had heard a great deal of the sinful tendency of men, but had not like some grown cynical or hard-hearted. There were others who pulled away from *Qayin*, some spit on the ground and made a clucking sound of despising; others turned their backs. But this officiating *kohen* did not. I watched his eyes closely. They seemed to me to be filled with pain and compassion. He moved toward *Qayin* attempting to comfort him and was soon streaked with lamb's blood himself.

Qayin, his beard virtually caked with the darkened red, resinous gummy mixture of lamb's blood, tears and limestone dust was so still, exhausted, strangling in the overwhelming sense of the consequences of his actions, afraid of what would happen next, and then after that and then after that. I think of the songs we sang in the Temple a few days ago. *Qayin's* soul was being pounded by chaotic destructive waves of fears, shame, guilt, despair, and anger at himself; or perhaps that is where I suspect that my heart would drive me.

In the normal non-priestly *'olah*, it is for the supplicant to perform the hand-leaning, the slaughtering, the quartering and the washing. It is only then that the *kohen* takes over and completes the *'olah*. This is so that the individual supplicants are intimately involved in the justice and mercy of G_d at a hands-on level. The supplicant has come up *lipne Elohim* for official court business. They are publicly admitting guilt, publicly admitting that the gates of the Garden of Eden have closed on them again due to their own choices and actions. They cannot take it anymore and want time turned back on the crime and its long trail of consequences. They long to be restored to the ones they hurt, the ripped fabric of the community rewoven and lastly, they long to be restored to the intimacy of G_d. And so they personally become involved in their own trial, verdict, and substitutionary death.

But it became clear to all of us who had gathered that *Qayin* emotionally just could not continue. The *kohen*, recognizing that *Qayin* could not perform his appointed role in the *'olah* grabbed the knife from *Qayin's* bloody hand and continued the work on *Qayin's* behalf. The *kohen* became *Qayin* the supplicant. He swiftly and skillfully chopped the lamb's head off, skinned and quartered the body, gathered the entrails up and washed them in the nearest laver. Then he brought the prepared body parts to the altar, with the exception of the skin and burned them to G_d as an *'olah* on *Qayin's* behalf. *Qayin* still would not look up, or move from his prostrate position, face on the ground, facing the *Holy Place*. He could only moan that he had forsaken *Elohim* and brought corruption into his household and pollution into the Temple.

The *kohen* walked back to the place where *Qayin* was prostrated and said to him, "*Qayin*, with this lamb, you are become clean before G_d. This lamb is a ransom for you to pay for all of your crimes against G_d. In the eyes of G_d, you are clean. It is finished." (I confess that my first thought was 'even <u>this</u> emaciated lamb?')

It appeared to me that the *kohen*'s proclamation was little encouragement to *Qayin*. Legally it is no doubt true that his crime had been mysteriously dealt with *lipne Elohim*. He was no longer subject to *G_d's* wrath for his pre-meditated crime. But in his own eyes, it seemed to me, there still was only unwashed darkness that blinded him, the swirling costs and consequences of his crimes. Then of course there is the consequence to the Temple of *G_d*, which *Qayin* dearly loved and had sought to serve his entire life.

All sins pollute the Temple, even sins that one commits daily unaware in their ignorance. But the brazen sin of a *kohen*? Surely that pollutes the very inner sanctuary and must be purged and cleansed quickly. Only the great purification offering done by the *High Kohen* on the *Day of Atonement* will suffice.

Still no movement, no acknowledgement; it was as if *Qayin* was dead. The *kohen* paused, tears formed in the corner of his eyes, and he instructed a number of the *kohanim* who had not turned away from *Qayin* to assist him home.

All knew that there was still much to be done. The elders must get involved to investigate, do appropriate due diligence, to determine what crimes were done, and what compensation would be required to restore monetarily what was wrongly taken. Clearly, covenants were broken. Clearly many have experienced a severe loss. Wisdom needs to be accessed in the community by all involved. What will now happen to the young couple? What is to be done concerning the betrothal contract? What is to be done with *Qayin's* family? What is to be done with *Qayin*? Or the groom-to-be? Or his family? What is to be said about the foolish woman, and of course the innocent young fruit of their lust in her unmarried womb? It is a terrible thing when a *kohen* succumbs to such crimes. The reconciliations will require the glory of *Adonai* Himself.

But I said to my heart, *Qayin* knows, or at least he used to know that such a redemptive restorative power exists. He too was present two years ago when *Adonai*'s glory entered the Temple. He did know once how entire communities can be healed from such a tear in the very foundational fibers.

But I also wonder, maybe this is the very reason that *Qayin* is so distraught. Only one who has truly experienced the *kabod* of *Adonai* can truly experience the agony of the opposite end of the spectrum: the stark absence of the glory of G_d in his heart. *Ichabod* indeed! He would not only feel guilt, and shame as a regular ignorant sinner might, but he would also feel a heightened sense of the alienation that comes when G_d's Spirit is experientially ripped from you. He would feel forsaken, as Adam and Eve did before him as they stood at the outside gate of Eden knowing that they could not go back in.

But *Yom Kippur* is coming.

THE JESIAH SCROLLS

9

The Nature of Justice

***Jesiah's* Journal Entry #9-**
The *Fifth of Tishri*- After Evening Prayers

Since I spoke to *Hevel*, I have spent most of my time reflecting on the current crisis within the ranks of the *kohanim*. So have other *kohanim*. There is a heavy death-like pall on the Temple campus. Part of me doesn't want to think about it anymore. *Qayin* was untaintable—or so we thought. What does this say about us? Our hearts? Or even more importantly: how does this corruption so close to the *Holy Place* affect G_d's favor toward Israel?

I had been very focused this year upon the question of what we are to feel on these days. But now, I can only think about justice. This was a horribly wicked betrayal. What could possibly begin to pay back such a crime? Who is wise enough to do such complex due diligence? Who can calculate the cost of such disrupted lives? Who can put a price on a child out of wedlock? Or the soiled career of a life-long *kohen*? Or to pay for such a betrayal of a sacred betrothal? The Holy Scrolls provide guidelines for *'asham* offerings in addition to *'olah*. It is just not enough for a person who has hurt another to merely make an offering to G_d in private. This would be another belittling of the other, wouldn't it?

Such an offering alone would really not reflect, in and of itself, a deep renewed concern for the one they wounded. G_d, who created all in their mother's womb has also discerned a path for forgiveness and reconciliation. It is not to say that anything at all is lacking in the work of the *Day of Atonement*. Reconciliation must also require that the perpetrator bring appropriate restitution in order to begin to re-honor the one they dishonored. For instance, in the Third Scroll of Moses, we read

"If anyone sins and is unfaithful to the Lord by deceiving his neighbor about something entrusted to him or left in his care, or stolen, or if he cheats him…"

Well, you get the idea.

"…When he thus sins and becomes guilty…"

And by this we understand the Prophet to be saying that the offender has been illuminated and is aware of what he did and he feels guilt and desires to reconcile,

"…he must return what he has stolen or taken by extortion, or what was entrusted to him, or the lost property he found, or whatever it was he swore falsely about. He must make restitution in full, add a fifth of the value to it and give it all to the owner on the day he presents his guilt offerings. And as a penalty, he must bring to the priest, that is, to the Lord his guilt offering, a ram from the flock, one without defect and of the proper value. In this way the priest will make atonement for him before the Lord, and he will be forgiven for any of those things he did that made him guilty."[xviii]

From this we understand that once illuminated, the offender should begin a long public process to regain fellowship with the one they dishonored. For that to occur, they must do whatever is right to restore the person to their former wealth or status, and then to pay a penalty which recognizes that crimes are not merely financial, but also losses of honor and glory. And so they pay a gift, not begrudgingly, which publicly honors their former victim, and in some way begins to restore the dignity that was robbed from them.

It is only then that the victim truly can move toward their former offender. It is commanded then that they should forgive the <u>repentant</u> perpetrator and move toward their brother or sister to embrace them. Of course this could take time humanly speaking, but for them to delay would be an additional crime. The *shalom* of the community is at stake.

But how can such a measure be determined? What is 'proper' value? We must rely on the righteous elders, the leaders of the community, village, city, or other wise officials to do the proper due diligence, hear the complaints and to make a determination which is fair and right. As I said, the ultimate goal is the full restoration of fellowship and community. *G_d* desires *shalom* for all aspects of the family of Israel.

As I wandered the Temple courtyard earlier, I was keenly aware of the growing number of supplicants who are bringing to the Temple very costly *'asham* only a few days before the *Day of Atonement*. They are seeking reconciliation with others. Though I did not see the woman involved in the scandal, I am told by a reliable source that she came at first light to the Temple with an *'asham*. She was by all accounts also quite ashamed and devastated at her part in the affair. Like *Qayin*, she has freely submitted her case to the elders for their judicial wisdom. But the whole affair has dampened the preparations for the upcoming festivities.

No doubt we will see an even greater activity of this after the *Day of Atonement*. Some say it is because when people see the covenantal kindness of *Adonai* toward them, their hearts are illumined so much that they can at last begin to see clearly how they have wounded others for the first time. I would say, though no doubt it is obvious, it is the kindness of the Lord that leads to repentance.

THE JESIAH SCROLLS

I am moved by the flurry of reconciliation activity. It is a glorious thing to imagine families restored, business partners hugging, crying and laughing, a fitting preparation for the joy that is to be experienced by all of Israel at *Sukkoth*. But still I wonder what practical hope there is for *Qayin* and the woman.

10

Qayin and *Hevel*

Now the man knew his wife Eve, and she conceived and bore Qayin,
saying, "I have gained a male child with the help of the LORD."
She then bore his brother Hevel.
Hevel became a keeper of sheep, and
Qayin became a tiller of the soil.
(Genesis 4:1-2 JPS with modifications)

Jesiah's Journal Entry #10- The *Tenth of Tishri-*
After Evening Convocation and Prayers

It was *Hevel!*

I still can't believe my ears. It was *Hevel!*

Hevel was the young priest who had been betrayed by *Qayin* and his
own betrothed. I still have a difficult time accepting it. Without
even knowing it, I have become embroiled in the matter by an act
of *Elohim.*

   Hevel! O my dear friend!

THE JESIAH SCROLLS

I wondered in my heart when he knew—when he found out. I don't remember seeing him in the Temple courts the day of *Qayin's 'olah*. Was *Qayin* the one that *Hevel* had to hurry off to meet the last time we were together? How poor a friend I have been. The irony has not been missed by the other astute priests: once again *Qayin* (Cain) has murdered his brother *Hevel* (Abel)!

I was told that when *Hevel* got the bad news, he said nothing— just turned and ran out the door and off of the Temple campus. That was over 24 hours ago. No one knew where he was. None of the *Sons of Asaph* had any idea. Some said that he spent some time with *Azariah* for counsel—but maybe that was wishful thinking. Others said that he went south, even as far as the Great River of Egypt. One person said that they heard that he was going after *Qayin*. Revenge.

Oh *Hevel*, I am so sorry! Personally, I was afraid of the worst— that he might try to take his own life. I don't know how I would handle such a tragic betrayal and loss, a death of a vision.

But I know now that *Hevel* had not done any of those things— he had considered revenge, but instead had run out to the wilderness—the broad harsh lifeless expanse just east of the city. The wilderness is a dry and barren place, inhospitable to humans. He said that he just 'went'. He wasn't thinking, or planning, or anything of the sort. He just went. Maybe it was to just die there. He wasn't sure. It would have been very easy to die there. There are no trees to protect you from the merciless sun. There are very few sources of water unless you can make it all the way to *En Gedi*, by the western bank of the Dead Sea, a hard day's journey. It is a good place for violated people to just go somewhere to die.

For *Hevel*, it turned out not to be a place of death, but rather a place where he could rage at the top of his voice to *G_d*. He told me that before he left the city, in the providence of *G_d* he happened to go past the small home of the aged and highly respected Levite, *Heman* the Kohathite. *Hevel* said that without any forethought or planning (hardly like *Hevel*) he just started desperately banging on the thick wooden door that led into the modest single roomed house of *Heman*. *Heman* was a legend among the priesthood. He was given the great honor of being called "The Singer" due to long and great service to David and to his son Solomon. He was long past his prime, in ill health and almost never saw visitors. But for reasons known only to himself, he agreed to give the despondent *Hevel* an audience. This was providential.

Heman is known for being very deep, and very transparent. His music is not the happiest collections of songs in Israel—in fact they are often quite dark, filled with rage and anger—not irreverent or disrespectful to *G_d*—but very, very honest. Many have criticized some of the starkest parts. *Heman* is unrepentant.

Apparently, *Heman* said very little to *Hevel*. He just let him cry and yell out. After a couple of hours he gave him a large plain scroll; an extensive collection of some of his dark worship songs. This was a *G_d*-send for *Hevel*.

Hevel said to me later that the particular songs on this scroll gave him words and gave him voice to truly express his pain and anger to *G_d*'s throne. They gave him permission to be, at least for a time, one of the many verbal waves of *Chaos* that were pounding on *G_d*'s throne this season. For a philosopher musician, this was perfect. May *G_d* richly bless *Heman* for his graciousness. He probably saved the life of my dear friend.

Later *Hevel* told me that one song in particular grabbed his heart and squeezed a well of poison out of him. He just repeated aloud to *G_d* it over and over again,

O Lord, the *G_d* who saves me, day and night
I cry out before you.
May my prayer come before you;
Turn your ear to my cry.
For my soul is full of trouble and
My life draws near the grave.
I am counted among those who go down to the pit;
I am like a man without strength.
I am set apart with the dead,
Like the slain who lie in the grave,
Whom you remember no more,

89

THE JESIAH SCROLLS

Who are cut off from your care.
You have put me in the lowest pit,
In the darkest depths.
Your wrath lies heavily upon me;
You have overwhelmed me with all your waves.

Selah

You have taken from me my closest friends and
Have made me repulsive to them.
I am confined and cannot escape;
My eyes are dim with grief.
I call to you, O Lord, every day;
I spread out my hands to you.
Do you show your wonders to the dead?
Do those who are dead rise up and praise you?

Selah

Is your love declared in the grave,
Your faithfulness in Destruction?
Are your wonders known in the place of darkness, or
Your righteous deeds in the land of oblivion?
But I cry to you for help, O Lord;
In the morning my prayer comes before you.
Why, O Lord,
Do you reject me and hide your face from me?
From my youth I have been afflicted and close to death;
I have suffered your terrors and am in despair.
Your wrath has swept over me;
Your terrors have destroyed me.
All day long they surround me like a flood;
They have completely engulfed me.
You have taken my companions and loved ones from me;
The darkness is my closest friend.

I caught up to *Hevel* shortly after the evening prayers. The day
of prescribed fasting had begun. I was wearing the coarse tunic
suitable for *innui nefesh*. I could honestly say that I am not
enamored with the outward appearance of fasting. I wonder if too

much attention is put on the garments. But still, in spite of that, I find the prescriptions helpful to maintain a reverent focus on the season.

I was restless. I was very concerned about *Hevel* and his well-being—but there was nothing for me to do. I was very nervous about the events of the Holy day tomorrow, troubled by the gross sins that have caused a violent and unsettling tear among the *kohanim* this year.

I wanted to leave the Temple proper and so I went down to the pool of *Siloam* on the southern tip of David's city. This is where the *kohanim* go to gather water for all Temple rituals. There I thought that I could think and order my thoughts regarding *Tamarah, Hevel* and *Qayin* and the *Day of Atonement.*

Qayin has been noticeably absent from the regular Temple activities. He has been relieved of all responsibilities. The affair has been turned over to the Elders of the Temple for trial, resolution and justice, so no one dares to say anything. They have been behind closed doors in the Temple gate for many hours now. I have a feeling of dread. Never before in my lifetime have such admissions come from a *kohen* of the character and righteousness as *Qayin*. This deeply troubles me. I dare not look too much into my inner thoughts. It may be destructive to me as well.

To my surprise I noticed the long-lost *Hevel* sitting cross-legged on the southern side of the ornate pool. His face was badly burnt by the wilderness sun; painfully so it looked to me. His hair was unkempt, and wet—matted down. He was a mess; but I was so glad to see him alive.

He was caught up in his thoughts, a very serious, even pensive look on his brow. He looked very much alone there. I wondered where his thoughts and feelings were taking him? Was he consumed by anger? Self-pity? Revenge? Betrayal is so very powerful. I did not know if I should disturb him. I did not know what I could possibly say to him. I had almost decided to slowly walk away, but he looked up and saw me. I could see some surprise, I think. Perhaps even a look of relief? I cannot be sure. He motioned slowly for me to come and sit with him.

For the next few minutes, there was only an unpleasant silence between us. It was *Hevel* who at last broke the silence. He smiled—or at least it appeared to me to be a smile, flicked a small pebble into the pool and glanced my direction, not with his whole face, but with his swollen fatigued eyes. I did sense that he was glad that I was there. It was then that he told me about his time with *Heman* and the scroll of 'venting songs' he called them—and the 'dark song' in particular that had enfleshed his loss, pain and rage in words. It had been a very painful 24 hours for my friend. He then let me in on his current ponderings,

"Do you remember, the other day, when you asked what are we to <u>feel</u> on these days? I have been asking myself that question over and over. I am sure that by now you know of my loss, the vile betrayal against me by one that I loved and another whom I considered a father. So now the question takes on new texture, a new heaviness, a poignant relevance. What are we to feel on this day, you ask? This is not merely a legal question of point of law anymore, is it? Oh no! This is <u>the</u> question of the day."

"Please allow me to speak to you honestly from my heart, for now is not the time for masks or looking good. On this holy day, I think, we are to begin to feel the birth pangs of a mixture of competing waves of chaotic emotions. This should <u>normally</u> be a time of great joy. It is our hope and heritage that G_d is Lord of the entire universe and is concerned with justice and consolation. Today, G_d is officially seated on His judgment throne, and from that vantage point can see all disorder in all of the cosmos. This is stunning news, particularly for those who have known great loss and injustice over the last twelve months or even the last twelve hours."

He paused. I could not tell if he was being forthright or cynical at this point. I assumed the former. *Hevel* tossed another small black oblong basalt stone into the pool causing a sizeable splash to leap up from the water. His haggard head was still not lifted up, his tired eyes now blankly focused on the point where the stone entered the now disrupted water which single-mindedly struggled to cover up the alien violation. I noticed again how the drought had affected the city. The water level in the pool was noticeably low.

Then *Hevel* again turned to me but this time with a glare on his face. I did not sense that he was angry at me; but he was angry nonetheless. He emphatically blurted out,

"*Jesiah*, who among us has no unresolved complaint, no formal charges to make against others on this day? Who among us has not been dishonored, mistreated, overlooked, robbed, offended, slandered, betrayed, the many things that men, even implacable *kohanim* do to each other? Is it not our hope that in a matter of days, there can be restoration to wholeness in Israel?"

His raised voice captured the attention of much of the crowd that was passing by the pool. He paused again, took a deep, deep breath and continued in a much more subdued serious tone.

"I must keep trying to imagine this. It is supposed to be a happy ending for victims."

"But this is where my ravaged heart dwells at this moment, my friend," he said as he looked directly at my face, "I must tell you just how desperately I want vindication and <u>real</u> justice. My rage is like a closed well which cries to be opened up and released. Those close to me have betrayed me. My heart demands justice, punishment and re-creation."

He moved a bit in place to find something more comfortable, perhaps his legs had fallen asleep. He drew one knee all the way up to his chest and held it there.

"But I must tell you also that I am aware of an ambivalence that deeply haunts my mind, an ambivalence that seeks to judge between competing movements in my soul. It is written that each one of us has not only suffered this year, but also has been an agent of *Chaos* against *G_d* and *G_d's* creation. It is true, it was not I who betrayed a betrothed. But who among us has consistently treated others as honorable image bearers of *G_d*? Who has truly loved? Who has not hurt others? Who among us has honored all of their vows, has been really faithful? Who has not betrayed, or complained as our forefathers did in the wilderness. Who among

93

us has been faithful to *G_d* as Abraham was, or for that matter even more faithful than last year?"

"I will tell you, my dear friend, that I have raging competitors in my heart. Part of my heart singularly wants vengeance and payback and will not be dislodged from its rabid mission. I do want justice. I want the perpetrator punished severely. It <u>will</u> be so. The perfect *G_d* will hear <u>all</u> cases against <u>each</u> of us on this day. He overlooks no crime. This is a scary thing, a nightmare for offenders. But if the truth were known, each of us comes to court on this day, both defendant and plaintiff. The only robe we don't wear on this day is the robe of the Judge. None of us has been our brother's keeper."

"That is what I was speaking to you about, shortly before my fragile order became *Chaos*. Our forefathers at the base of *Sinai* did not know what to feel and were led into gross error. We would do well to avoid their path. Yet I am consumed with self-focused, confusion and the rage of a slave, not a *kohen* of *G_d*. I am in pain. I am forsaken."

His last words echoed in my mind, reminding me of another cry—another recent voice.

He paused, looked out over the horizon and sighed deeply. It was dark now. Since it was the time of the New Moon, the only lights were few torches or oil lamps scattered about. He took another deep cleansing breath and re-engaged his argument. His voice was not strong, but broken. He spoke, not fluidly, but rather in emotional clumps, struggling to maintain some scholarly visage.

I am very much aware, as I try to faithfully transcribe my friend's powerful feelings and words, that I am falling quite short in capturing the deeper hurt that he expresses in his un-*Hevel*-like movements, his diverted eyes, his broken voice patterns, the long pauses, the erratic jumbled thoughts. He continued.

"Yes, that is a good analogy, I think. The Israelite who has come to Jerusalem on the holy days of *Tishri* in obedience is very much like our forefathers who came to *Sinai*. Both came per the command of *Adonai*. Both have spent a period in oppressive enslavement. For our forefathers, this is obvious. For us? Isn't it evident to the bright among us that we have spent eleven months in a variety of enslavements to a variety of masters, some cruel, some oppressive, some self-inflicted. Like our forbearers, we had grown comfortable as slaves. We have learned how to try to manipulate the powers, to bend the fates, to make do, and in some cases <u>do</u> pretty well. We would really rather not admit this, but our community looks much like the community of the pagan gods; self-centered, ambitious, independent lovers of self (or haters of self—just a variant of the former) more than they love anyone else. For slaves, relationships are, for the most part tools, useful to make life bearable. But intimacy is strained at best, in many cases scarred beyond normal repair. One person uses another, blames others…betrays others. Where does one find hope?"

The normally rational, very controlled *Hevel* was becoming more agitated again and visibly both saddened and disturbed. He was now speaking from the depths of a wounded soul, not just of his mind. His usual lightness and playfulness was displaced by a somber tightness. His words were less well chosen for exactness and more for emphasis. He was not sure at this moment what he was supposed to feel.

"You may be tempted to think that I am overstating my case, that I need to get out of the Temple more often. Maybe I see the worst in humanity. It is not necessary for me to establish anything more than this. Even our best relationships, our very, very best fall tragically short of the intimacy and community that we were designed for in *Adonai*. We come to the *Day of Atonement*… <u>every one</u> of us with multiple scars, debts, injustices and wounds. We are a people who <u>desperately</u> need justice and justice's healing. We each need a spotless unmottled sufficient ram as an *'olah* for us. Our relationships are far from the free and vulnerable intimacy enjoyed and explored by Adam and Eve before the fall. We can deny it of course. Denial is part of our protective mechanism, I fear. But denial is not our friend here *lipne Elohim*. He certainly can see through our cover-ups, our self-made lies, whether we believe them or not. *Adonai* has proclaimed in His compassion that every crime committed against us…"

Here *Hevel* stopped in his tracks as if something had taken his breath away. He dropped his face. His visage darkened not with anger I thought, but rather it was a moment of emotional pain. I imagine now as I write this that poor *Hevel* was at that moment being pounded internally by a vast wave made up of a complex interweaving of emotions: hurt, betrayal, violation of trust, love and future lost, a hopelessness, maybe even doubt and cynicism in any goodness, any consistency. This wave rose up and for a brief time enveloped him whole. The great mind blinded in a flash of darkness. Extended moments passed. There was even more awkward silence. *Hevel* finally shook his head as if to clear away any unwanted thoughts or emotions, or maybe to counter any remnant of fatigue.

"Oh, *Jesiah*! I lost my train of thought. I am truly undone..."

He splashed water from the pool upon his face and rubbed his reddened eyes and continued.

"This I know to be so very true. Every crime committed against each of us this year will get His full attention until it is perfectly resolved and what was taken or withheld from us is returned. *G_d* loves us that much and will not rest until perfect justice is accomplished. All things bent will be made straight."

Doves had discovered us at last and swooped down near us, waddling on the steps behind and before us begging for scraps of bread. *Hevel* was unmoved by their plight. He, quite deliberately I thought, stood erect, tossed another stone in the pool quite near where the last one disappeared. The doves scattered to other parts of the courtyard. I wondered to myself if he wanted to avoid speaking directly about *Tamarah*. Without turning his head, he began again.

"I remember now. Back to our emotions. What should we <u>feel</u> as we come to these days? And particularly this year? This is a frightening thing. I mean this in the most human sense. This is a chilling thing to come immediately into His audience as He rises to His throne to hear <u>all</u> cases in the universe. When we were safe in our homes, distanced from the powerful presence of *G_d* as Judge, we were managing reasonably well in our lives. Slaves know how to manage things well, heroically perhaps, and yet remain slaves. But the closer we come to G_d, we see afresh the annual amnesia clears and we see that we have been tragic slaves, gross fools, celestial underachievers and vile offenders to each other. We remember that we are called by Him to be His children of glory and promise, His beloved, His glorious ones. But the closer we come, the more lost and alone we feel. Like our *Sinai* forbearers and like Adam, our shame grabs us. Shame is a deep-seated self-hatred that failures experience. We have wasted another year going our own way, wandering like stupid sheep, willingly, foolishly, and yes, ignorantly. The closer we come to His presence the more like failures we feel. The whole community reeks with our destructive ways. The Temple is horribly soiled by the putrid consequences of our sins."

"But the closer we come, the greater is our sense of personal loss; a growing sense of how abusively we have been treated by others, those who were charged to honor us."

He paused, turned away. I thought that I heard his voice choke up again which caused the same phenomenon in me. I was very affected by his suffering, his discomfort, with his struggle to find a way out of his confusion. I also felt a very strange sense that I was eavesdropping on someone's very personal, very private conversation. I did not dare to say anything.

"Slaves have to discount themselves and their value. People regularly treat them poorly. The rational mind— and slaves are, if anything, rational animals— must come up with an explanation for such treatment by so many 'others'. The only logical explanation (or at least at the time the only logical explanation) is that we are not worth being treated well. Masterpieces of great craftsmen are treated with great care, not trash tossed away in the road only to be trampled on by donkeys and dogs. *Hevel*, today I feel like trash."

"There is great benefit to this natural trajectory for victims, for if we begin to really believe that we are without value and without worth, then mistreatment loses its pain to us. Then, it can be reasonably and rationally justified as normal. In fact, it is the pain that must be reasoned away as unreasonable. The person becomes trash. But on this day, *Adonai* gathers such trash around Himself. The closer we come to *Adonai*, and we meditate on the story, the *Sacred Scrolls*, the more we remember that we are masterpieces by nature, not slaves—not trash; that we are Princes and Queens, not slugs. *Lipne Elohim* the pain of all of the wounds is resurrected in a flurry of agony, often unbearable."

Hevel then raised his balled fist into the air firmly and raised his voice even higher as if he were speaking to a larger invisible audience. All heads turned to our direction again.

"What do I feel? On this high day? My heart wants immediate justice for the crimes against me. I want what was taken from me restored. I want the person who violated *Tamarah* to be punished publicly for what he did to me, to us, to our families, to our tribe. I want justice! I want an explanation of choices from *Tamarah*. I want to know why?"

His voice tailed off, his head dropped again, his shoulders heavy and slumped forward. He took some more deep labored breaths, perhaps to slow down his racing pulse. Then he calmly began again.

"But here is what also troubles me to my bones. Alongside my rage, my just complaints to *G_d*, my loss, my betrayal, I feel this too. As I prepare to go up to the Temple, *lipne Elohim*, I am more and more aware that I too have committed multiple crimes... innumerable crimes against others. I have this in common with *Qayin* and *Tamarah*. We both have been Egypt to our friends and family. We are all perpetrators. We have used others for our selfish purposes, to make great edifices and reputation for ourselves at their expense. We have coveted what others have. We have defrauded others, withheld what was due them. We have burdened others to serve ourselves. We have not loved as we could have. We have not raised others up, lifted their reputations, or honored them at every opportunity. We are all guilty and will all stand before *G_d* without a defense, with no possible way for us to repay such mistreatment to other masterpieces; at least to the point that *G_d* would be satisfied. We would have to turn the clock back to last year and re-do the year. This is not within the power of man under the sun. We will in a few days stand before the Holy Tribunal and hear His voice, the same voice that proclaimed order in the primordial *Chaos*, publicly say over them, and me, 'GUILTY!'"

He cried out the last word at the very top of his lungs.

"GUILTY! Guilty! *Jesiah*, I have come to realize this day, that I <u>too</u> have spent eleven months as an agent of *Chaos*, in foolish hubris working functionally against *G_d* and His Kingdom. He desires a single unified people; but we have sought our own glory over others. He desires faithfulness and righteousness. We could only think of <u>our</u> own lusts, our plans, reputations and coffers. Our crimes are foundationally the rebellion of unbelief, not so very different from the seminal illicit reach of unbelief committed by our Mother Eve and Father Adam. Only we have done it regularly, daily, under the mask of righteousness, religious service and even ministry to *G_d*. We come to the Great King over all the Universe who sees all, who hates sin, who promises that there will be no crime overlooked."

"We sing, 'The Lord reigns, let the nations tremble.' And it is so for our knees as well. Amen."

"You my friend have indulged my thoughts and ramblings on what men feel when they come before the face of the living *G_d*. But one of our Temple songs describes it so well in metaphor. I will suffer you to hear me sing the piece, for this is what I have been trained to do. Many worshippers feel a deep connection with the words, some before they come to this day. For others, the sense overcomes them during the ten days. This is part of the plan of redemption of our Lord."

Then through his tears and clearly fighting back more, he still melodically began to sing these words so poignantly, so wonderfully. He clearly was moved by the words—these were his very soul-words—this was *Hevel*.

Some lost their way in the wilderness,
In the wasteland;
They found no settled place.

Hungry and thirsty, their spirit failed.

Some lived in deepest darkness,
Bound in cruel irons,
Because they defied the word of G_d,
Spurned the counsel of the Most High.

He humbled their hearts through suffering;
They stumbled with no one to help.

There were fools who
Suffered for their sinful way,
And for their iniquities.
All food was loathsome to them;
They reached the gates of death.

Others go down to the sea in ships,
Ply their trade in the mighty waters;
They have seen the works of the LORD and
His wonders in the deep.

By His word He raised a storm wind that made the waves surge.
Mounting up to the heaven,
Plunging down to the depths,
Disgorging in their misery,
They reeled and staggered like a drunken man,
All their skill to no avail.

In their adversity they cried to the LORD, and
He saved them from their troubles.

Let them praise the LORD for His steadfast love,
His wondrous deeds for mankind.
Let them exalt Him in the congregation of the people,
Acclaim Him in the assembly of the elders.[xix]

"Are you familiar with the trumpet accompaniment to this song? No? You really should hear it when the choirs have gathered to sing it. Tears flow like the well that feeds this pool. By the way, the hymn ends with *Adonai* alone, unilaterally, providing salvation to His people. Praise be to our Lord *G_d*."

"In this season, we <u>must</u> draw near, victim and perpetrator alike, for who can perfectly distinguish between the two? We must come together *lipne Elohim*. We feel many different things: anger, hatred and vengeance... perhaps joy, fear, sadness as well. We are all charged to wait, to be still, quiet. We all hear the same rumbles and thunder of the voice of *G_d* from the Mountain. For us it is the quiet thunder of *G_d's* presence and conviction. We wait, knowing full well what the verdict will be. How can it be otherwise?"

Hevel slowly rose to his feet, not as a young man filled with energy, but rather as a slumped shouldered much older man. He just stood there gazing, empty of tears for the moment; staring frozen-eyed across the expansive pool, quiet. Maybe he became aware that he was rambling in his words. Normally *Hevel's* thoughts were so linear and organized. But his thoughts this day were quite chaotic. I am not criticizing him at all. I would not dare to. I also noticed—it is strange what one observes in awkward moments— that the pool was perfectly still where the rock had entered just a moment before. It was as if nothing had happened.

"This is what I feel, my friend. May *G_d* lift the burden of injustice that I carry this day, along with its adulterous mistresses self-righteousness, anger, and rage."

Hevel had finished. It was as if he was a broken cistern that had finally finished spilling out its content. He now appeared quite tired. We embraced as true brothers and then I left him alone again with his thoughts, as heavy as they seemed. It seemed to me that before this pool, *Hevel* was indeed *lipne Elohim* in a way that I could not understand.

THE JESIAH SCROLLS

As I now write all of my recollection of the evening I want to try to record my confused feelings at this point. I normally am able to follow *Hevel's* logic, even at its most brilliant heights. I am usually able to relate to my friend. But not tonight! I am not at all comfortable with the turn in the conversation. I do not fully understand his ambivalence. It was a *high handed* crime against him. I am still angry <u>for</u> him. I have not spent 24 hours in the wilderness with a scroll of songs that vent to *G_d*. I am still in shock. For me, the lines that *Hevel* spoke of, between victim and perpetrator were far too blurred. Imprecise. It was *Qayin* who was the perpetrator here, not *Hevel*. What *Qayin* did to my friend *Hevel* was horrific and *high handed* and must be dealt with severely, and soon. This is a holy time, and this crime has soiled everything that it stands for.

I can see that I have prepared myself for the usual ongoing generic waves of *Chaos* smashing against the throne of *G_d* <u>from the outside</u>. But this year, a vile new unexpected wave has crashed upon us all apparently <u>from the inside</u>. For *Hevel* to bend down to identify with the heart motives of the one who belittled him so much, who treated him so badly is, frankly, very offensive to me. I am very angry… and I feel righteous judgment against *Qayin*.

I don't know where *Hevel* is going with his logic. I am disrupted more than I have been for a long time. But the worst feeling of all is that I feel somehow marginalized from my friend. I can't explain it but I feel a wave of loneliness inside. It is as if I have lost him somehow. I wonder if *Heman's* dark song echoes much of what each *kohen* (including me) is feeling today.

[The souls of the kohanim are] full of trouble and
[Our corporate] life draws near the grave.
[We are] counted among those who go down to the pit;
[We are] without strength.
[We are] set apart with the dead,
Like the slain who lie in the grave,
Whom you remember no more,
Who are cut off from your care.
You have put [us] in the lowest pit,

102

In the darkest depths.
Your wrath lies heavily upon [us];
You have overwhelmed [us] with all your waves.[xx]

Selah

Selah indeed!

The destructive waves of *Chaos* are not just from the outside this year—but rather from *G_d's* throne itself. It is as if *G_d* has ordained *Chaos* somehow? It sounds too absurd to be true—a speculation of a fool?

It is the New Moon and it is so very dark. On the way back to my cell, I noticed that 'King' Silas was dining on a huge flat bread. I can only shake my head and smile.

THE JESIAH SCROLLS

11

More Thoughts

Jesiah's Journal Entry #11

I just re-read my thoughts from last night—hoping that a night of sleep, even the restless night of broken sleep that I had would clear my head and help me to see a light in this confusion and darkness. But my heart is still very heavy. I feel as if I have not been a very good friend to *Hevel* but I also feel that I have nothing to say to him on the path that he is on.

As I pondered *Hevel's* earlier words, I have concluded that maybe the Holy season can be defined by its means and end. The end of the *High Holy Days* would be The Party on the *Fifteenth of Tishri*: the Great Feast of *Booths*, the wonderful celebration of *G_d* as the Provider to His people. But until there is a trial for every crime, sufficient justice for all injustices, and *G_d* Himself straightening what His image-bearers have bent, there can truly be no holy convocation of *Sukkoth*. For at *Sukkoth*, <u>all</u> Israel sits at a fellowship meal, shared by everyone. Until the broad spectrum of crimes have been fully and completely addressed, and the consequential shame, guilt, and fears are purified from the community, there can be no *shalom*. The harvest is not yet incomplete. Imagine enemies eating at the fellowship table. Imagine *Hevel* sitting alongside of *Qayin* and *Tamarah?* It seems to me that it would be a mockery of *G_d's* order and provision. Imagine victim and offender unresolved at *G_d's* table that He pays so dearly for. It is a crime of the highest order.

The 'means', then, would be the purification rituals that are part of the *Day of Atonement* on the *Tenth of Tishri.* Whatever happens at *Yom Kippur*, it must include the full payment of objective celestial justice. This must be experientially paid for every single crime committed over the year and also, equally important for *shalom's* purposes, the Holy Temple must be washed clean from all of the sins of all of Israel. And lastly, shame and guilt must somehow be washed off of and removed from all participants.

After these are accomplished, all that is left is for *Adonai* to infuse His renewed, reborn people with joy. Then let the party of *Booths* begin. I wondered in my heart if perhaps some of the raging waves of *Chaos* that challenge *G_d's* throne in the Coronation Psalms are the guilt and shame that are in the very hearts of Israel? But even I can't imagine a resolution to this year's tragedy.

What does *G_d* have in mind?

12

The Cleaning Crew

Jesiah's Journal Entry #12

Today, my team was on cleaning rotation. Normally, it is a job that I definitely don't care for. It is very smelly and hot, very filthy work. But I must confess, today I did not mind; anything to get my thoughts off of recent events and conversations.

Today, the usually burdensome task turned into a personal lesson from the heavens. It seems to me that the activities of the _High Kohen_ on the _Day of Atonement_ are in some ways like a strong detergent that purges all surfaces of anything that would hinder intimacy between _G_d_ and others. There is nothing that can clean away the stench of our crimes against each other—nothing. Humanly speaking of course. But once a year _G_d_ brings in a detergent powerful enough to clean us even of the vileness of the crimes of _Qayin_. Then and only then can we fully enjoy _Sukkoth_. Until that happens, _Sukkoth_ is only a façade, a ruse for pious actors. Let me try to explain.

On normal days, and much more so on Holy days with their multitude of sacrifices, the floor of the Temple court, and in particular the iron restraining loops become heavily stained with the thick gummy blood residue from the many offerings. If allowed to set in the fierce heat of the sun, the putrid stench can become so intolerable, that, not only does it attract a variety of rodents and bugs, but the supplicants can't come near the altar due to the oppressive smell and pollution. On some days the miasmas, the stench from the multitude of sin offerings seems to roll almost wavelike outside the Temple gates, seeping into even the lower court and causing no slight sicknesses among the pilgrims who have come to draw near to *G_d*. During one New Moon celebration—it was just last summer I think, the grates clogged up for a few days. The vile odor that resulted caused many worshippers and attendants to develop a wrenching sickness that lasted for days in some cases. We called it 'The Temple's Revenge.' Sin has consequences.

In order to avoid such an occurrence again, the priests are put on a rotating clean-up schedule. This happened to be my day.

To accomplish our task, there are bronze lavers dedicated to the production of industrial strength detergent specifically engineered to remove such pollution from the Temple floor. In the exclusive markets below us, soap is generally made from reacting expensive virgin olive oil with the ashes from burned Cassis tree bark. That soap would do us little good in our task, though the cinnamon smell would definitely be a welcomed relief. The task of removing the stain of sin from the Temple floor requires something far more powerful.

So specialists have learned that if you take ashes directly from the *Great Altar*, disperse them in a dedicated laver filled with water, and heat it to a boil; then take animal fat, from the many non-'*olah* offerings, add it to the boiling mixture, and continue to boil until the water is almost gone, you will end up with a detergent, that while it doesn't smell very pleasant— at all— the yellow slimy sludge will successfully remove even the worst of animal stains. The cleaning teams work the detergent into the worst areas with stiff brushes and scrapers. Then buckets of water are poured into the foamy mixture directing it toward one of the many grates in the Temple floor which subsequently lead to an ingeniously designed series of culverts which transport the polluted water away from the Temple Terrace, down alongside the western edge of the *Ophel,* even further down to the *Central Valley* moving the vile mix to the lowest point of the Valley of Hinnom, far away from the Temple of G_d so that it can in no way hinder those who want to come to be *lipne Elohim.*

The detergent is specifically engineered to remove even the worst built-up stench and sickening pollution that would in any way hinder our coming near to G_d and G_d's experiential favor from coming near to us. This is what will happen in a few days hence. On *Yom Kippur,* the spiritual detergent powerful enough to clean up the fiercely entrenched blood-stain that mars Israel will ironically be made of the blood of the sacrificed goat, not from its rendered fat.

I can't wait to share these thoughts with *Hevel.* He loves irony. All I need is a stale bread pointer.

According to the Holy Scrolls, all crimes of humanity, those against heaven, man, and creation, whether they are knowing or unknowing, large or small, in fact even those where *'olahs* have already been offered *lipne Elohim,* each and every one pollutes the Temple of G_d. It is as if every sin creates an unseen airborne pollution that seeps into the Temple and forms a vile patina on the places where *Adonai* is to dwell. Certainly it would be a very vile and *high handed* crime that would dare to violate the Holiest place and dare to land on the *Ark* cover itself. But this is so. And it seems to me that the crimes of this season fit that category! Amen?

It is also taught that, simply put, G_d, and all the power of G_d will not dwell in the midst of such vile pollution. Though He is indeed long-suffering, there comes a point where G_d will abandon His sanctuary and His people whom He loves (May G_d forbid!) and leave us exposed and at the disposal of the nations far greater than us.

But, it is also taught that there is a remedy given to us. Life-blood is the efficacious detergent that can clean pollution off of the Temple and restore it to 'holiness'. This is not to be understood as our pagan neighbors do, that the blood has some intrinsic detergent

109

capabilities which when multiplied by the ritual, along with incantations, sexual activities and chants empower the deity to defeat entities of *Chaos* that have infiltrated their inner chambers. Our sacrifices don't magically immunize the Temple. Nothing of the sort.

Let me put it another way. The hope of Israel is birthed out of our seminal narrative. It was *Adonai* Himself who drew near to, without becoming polluted by, the primordial formlessness and void; that lonely, disenfranchised alienated *Chaos*. His Spirit hovered over it, so close, so intimately that He could creatively speak into it; and yet he was totally unaffected by its filth. It is right to say that all of creation is birthed out of primordial pollution. The unlikely offspring of such a father and mother was all of the creation that we see: the sun, moon, stars, the sky, the sea, the great lands and islands, all fish in the sea, birds in the air, even the great monsters of the deep, and of course, mankind.

Behold it is so! For mankind, *Adonai* had a higher calling and purpose. We were to be His special creation, His *segullah*, His beloved. He breathed His breath into us alone and created a race of Kings and Queens who were to carry His banner to the edge of Eden and beyond. In His name and power, always *lipne Elohim*, we were charged to defeat the tragic Dame *Chaos* and her vile brood until there was none remaining.

It is important to say a word about Eden, the holiest of *Holy Places*. In Eden, mankind was more mankind than we can imagine now in this place so far east of Eden. It was not that we were taller, more handsome, or even more *G_d*-like; though the latter was no doubt the case. What made our race more human was that we were inseparable from *G_d* Himself.

How can I describe this heady thought? (Oh my, I can see that *Hevel* has begun to have a very positive effect on me. I am beginning to think and write like him. *Jesiah* the Prophetic? I think that I will stick with my *shofar*).

So how can I describe this heady '*Hevelian*' thought? In regular parlance, we speak of the family as a single indivisible social unit of measure. It is absurd to speak of an individual really. At the core, each of us is foundationally defined by, shaped by, identified by who we are as part of a specific family. I was born *Jesiah*, son of Menna. Nothing can ever separate me from who I am. But hear this! Adam was born Son of *Adonai*. He along with Eve was indivisible from *Adonai*. And now *Adonai* has chosen Israel, the second Adam, as a special people; and He dwells with her. I remember just two years ago, when we viscerally experienced what that means. This is not merely a philosophical bit of legal rhetoric, the language of written contract (e.g., "This day, I, the aforementioned undersigned now covenant to be the ally of the latter aforementioned, etc. etc…"). Not at all!

Hinneh! For us, *G_d*-with-us is identity and life. If *G_d* ever withdrew, we would be identity-less orphans, wanderers again in the wilderness, a tragic people of no name. For Adam and Eve, *G_d* not only dwelt among them, as He is with us this day, but Adam and Eve dwelt in His presence continually. I can only wonder what this could mean by implication and speculation for I have never felt such a thing for more than a moment of time. But it would certainly include a sense of self and intimacy within a community that I envy. It would be a Garden where there is no shame, no fears, no guilt, no betrayals, only life in abundance, dancing, giving to others—in a word, 'righteousness'. The Scrolls say it in this manner, "In the Garden they were naked and knew no shame." *Adonai* did not resign Himself to the Holiest of Holy places alone, but walked in the un-polluted camp among His glorious unpolluted people. My mind wonders at the possibility of such a time and place. I cannot bear the thought of such a thing but I equally can't bear the thought of that not happening again.

Today I performed my gross smelly duties with a very high spirit. The hot sun had already begun to harden much of the residue making it very hard to scrub off—much harder than usual. We put in a very long and hard day's work. I look forward to grabbing a couple hours of sleep on my cot. I am still angry at the events of recent days, but my mind is energized by these thoughts—and my spirit is greatly lifted. *G_d* really does have a plan that is higher than any of our plans. His justice then is also higher than our justice. He will not overlook any crime, any violation. There will, there must be justice.

I hope to return to this line of thought soon. Perhaps I am beginning to see and understand what *Hevel* was speaking of? Cleansing, external cleansing must happen today if there is to be any peace in Israel, particularly this year!

13

Abiathar's Thoughts

***Jesiah's* Journal Entry #13-**
The *Tenth of Tishri*- Midday

At last! Today is the *Tenth of Tishri*, the day provided by G_d for the purging of all sins of Israel, including all of the sins which each of us have done unaware, in ignorance, but also total purging for crimes which each of us has done knowingly.

Yesterday, still quite distraught over the *Qayin* affair, I made an appointment with the Sage, the man who is charged with overseeing the spiritual care of the Temple musicians. *Abiathar* is a very wise generous man, full of life, and equally full of great thoughtfulness. In some ways, he reminds me of an older and rounder *Hevel.* He was keenly aware of the recent troubles and had spent much time in prayer and meditation over the complicated matters.

I began by asking him if the purging of the day really did cleanse Israel and the Temple from all sins, <u>even</u> the *high handed* brazen ones. Of course I had the *Qayin* affair on my mind. My question was one of justice certainly. *Hevel* has been robbed blatantly, *high handedly*. It is hard to imagine how justice could ever restore what was taken. In the *Fifth Scroll*, the Prophet Moses says that anyone who does acts *high handedly* whether native-born or alien, blasphemes the Lord, and that person must be cut off from his people. Because he has despised the Lord's word and broken his commands, that person must surely be cut off; his guilt remains on him.[xxi]

Clearly there had been much discussion and concern about the *Qayin* affair throughout the Temple priesthood and staff. I was not the first to ask such a question. His answer was provocative,

"The Scrolls clearly proclaim that <u>all</u> of the sins of <u>all</u> Israel are atoned for this day. We take great solace in the written *Torah* instructions about these offerings, mentioned on no other occasion, that the atonement offered today is 'concerning all of our sins'. The Great King David was no doubt meditating on this grace of *Adonai* when he appealed to *G_d* to forgive his great *high handed* iniquity. He cried to *Adonai*, perhaps even on the *Day of Atonement*, '*The troubles of my heart have multiplied, free me from my anguish. Look upon my affliction and distress and take away <u>all</u> my sins.*'"

"And hear the same from the Great Levitical Choir of the Sons of *Korah*, 'O Lord, You will favor Your land, restore Jacob's fortune; You will forgive Your people's iniquity, pardon <u>all</u> their sins; Selah.[xxii]'"

"*G_d* is merciful beyond description, His faithfulness above the heavens. This is the brokenness of the man whom *G_d* hears and answers. He will be free from the guilt and shame of his crimes. He will enter into *Sukkoth* with a clean heart and righteousness will flow from him as from a full well, and joy will be his companion. But…."

He said as he raised his index finger high with a patented grandfatherly grin,

"…the *high handed* who knowingly commits a crime with forethought and malice and remains stiff-necked, who will <u>not</u> repent from the heart—ah, <u>that</u> person will not truly <u>experience</u> the purging provided for them. They cannot draw near to *Adonai*.

They must live experientially outside Eden by their own choice. They chose for themselves the path, the city of their spiritual father *Qayin*, which he built to escape from *G_d's* love after the murder of his brother *Hevel*."

Abiathar paused to collect his thoughts. I noticed that other priests had entered the room wanting to hear what he might say. They were so quiet that I had not heard them come in. *Abiathar* stood up, acknowledged each new person with a fatherly nod of his age-wizened face and continued his thoughts.

"Gentlemen, these Holy days are all about the restoration of intimacy with *G_d*; or better, the removal of the many things that have entered the garden of our intimacy and have caused either of us to be repelled by the vile pollution. May I take you back to the first place where our intimacy with *G_d* first suffered from such pollution? It seems to me that there was in our *Holy Place*, the Garden, a powerful shrewd entity of *Chaos*, which *G_d* mysteriously allowed to be there. It is a curious thing, that *G_d* allowed the source of pollution within the *Holy Place* of Eden: the Usurper, the Leaven-that-lives, the Accuser himself. We all know the tragic story of course; from youth we are told and retold the story. But my interest at this moment of reflection is what happened after the illicit reach of unbelief of *G_d's* first family. It was then that vile pollution was ushered back into the holy camp with the first family's and *G_d's* implicit permission. The success of the Serpent was that he convinced our parents that the formlessness and void, the loneliness and estrangement of *Chaos* was of a higher existence than Eden."

"Now something quite strange occurred, something that occurs daily in our time. The very persons who were created from the dark and lifeless womb of *Chaos*, who took their first breaths in abundant life in the arms of *Adonai*, willingly chose, through the art of deception, to re-enter the womb alienated and estranged from the one who had first given them birth and life."

"Of course we do this every time we choose *Chaos* over life; when we choose to go our own way; when we choose to look disdainfully on any aspect of *G_d's* creation, or His prescription and

115

Law; when we reach out with our derivative reach of unbelief and re-enter the lifeless and lonely womb of *Chaos*."

"In my mind, I go back to the scene immediately after the infamous first fruit. Can we not see the parallels to today's activities? Immediately all the pollution of *Chaos* rushed into the *Holy Place*, the place where *G_d's* specific *shekinah* intentionally and mysteriously not only dwelt, but the very marriage bed where He and His bride were bedded. The violent raging waves of *Chaos* polluted everything, all nooks and crannies, all of man's 'coming-ins' and 'going-outs'."

"What did it feel like? Our parents felt a deep, deep alienation from themselves, each other and the entire cosmos. It was as if for the first time the primal umbilical cord of humanity was violently severed. From that point on, we devolved from named persons into entities only slightly more valuable than the afterbirth from a woman's labor."

"Man's first awareness of alienation was from himself. It was at that shocking moment that our father and mother stopped seeing themselves as persons-in-relation with their perfect community and wholly defined themselves as objects-in-opposition to the other, highly exploitable. I am not a person <u>with</u> you, a 'who'; rather I am an object <u>for</u> you, a 'what', in fact a naked exposed 'what'. From that point, we no longer identified with the name *G_d* gave us, but began to define ourselves by other lesser adjectives due objects. I am 'naked' and 'not attractive'. I am 'strong'. I am a 'victim'. Or I am identified by what I 'want'. I want power, security, wealth, honor, sex. Remember the first son, the demanding-one *Qayin*, 'I am first born so I have… no, I demand certain rights'?"

"It was in our de-birth into *Chaos'* womb in which we truly become emotionally slaves. One of the first fruits of our slave-hearts is that now we demand payment for work. At best, now, we are only worth what we <u>do</u>, not whose we are."

"One must speculate about what *G_d* was purposing in the Garden as He gazed into the shadows of the trees (which, by the way, He had made <u>not</u> for himself but for Man) and said with a voice (which, by the way, he had created for communication with man), and in a language (which was also an accommodation for intimacy with man), and tragically asked a question that would be totally unnecessary before, 'Where are you, O Man?'"

As he stretched out the G_d-question no doubt for emphasis, *Abiathar* looked directly into the face of each man in the room. It elicited chuckles from the younger priests. He started using his hands and arms much more freely as props.

"One might venture that G_d really couldn't see them as the trees were in the way. But that would be absurd. One might also venture that G_d was beginning the speedy trial, and that this was the summons for the key witness and the key defendant, man. Perhaps. But...," he paused, "It is my conviction that by these words He is once again speaking into *Chaos* afresh, powerfully beginning to re-assemble the seminal fabric of order. It is the beginning of the rebirth of creation, the first pains of the second childbirth. It was not G_d who needed to know where man was. It was estranged man who was now in the undulating graspings of *Chaos'* womb."

"The question of G_d found Adam and Eve, now so polluted with such *Chaos* that they were no longer truly free agents. Burdened with such filth, they just could not approach the one they had only known previously in pure holy embrace. They could not freely gaze into the eyes that they long knew only as life-giving mirrors. They could only plead for protection from G_d's purity and holiness; they desperately grasped for any boundaries— as pathetic as leaves are for that purpose. Not just boundaries from G_d, but from each other of course and even within themselves, blindspots: the inner leaves that protected their spirits from the *Chaos* within. They could not, or better would not dare ask G_d for re-birth, for cleansing from their self-afflicted pollution. Maybe they were ignorant of G_d's eternal willingness to rebirth them, even seventy times seven times, if need be."

"For them, while it is correct to say that death and ejection from Eden was a punishment for their crime against G_d, it is far more on point to say that the ejection was the necessary beginning

117

of a long redemption process that would lead to their re-birth and restoration to Eden—from the experience of forsakenness to recovery of community."

While he was still speaking he walked over to the single window in the cell and pulled back the curtains. A very welcomed cool breeze wafted into the room. He put his forefinger thoughtfully to his chin, paused and returned to his lesson. All eyes were still very much upon him.

"These events are only the extended first act of the drama that is the *Day of Atonement*. As it happened then, *Chaos* has once again polluted the very inner court of the Holy of Holies. It has affected all that *G_d* loves. I make this point here at last. Note that *G_d* is never ever polluted by *Chaos*. No. He is far too large and glorious for that to occur. *Chaos* only pollutes creation. *G_d's* plan is to, as it was in the beginning, speak into the *Chaos* annually, at the *Day of Atonement* and re-create a garden and a people for Himself. And so since the first blast of the *shofar*, ten days ago, it is as if *G_d's* Spirit has been hovering over all of the *Chaos* that has seeped into Eden, into the community of man, of Israel in particular. And on this day, He *bara's* (creates) once again."

"It is on this day, that this is the work of *G_d* alone, not of man. Only *G_d* creates. What is our role? Our participation? It is for us to recognize by faith that we are, or better yet, we have become over the last twelve months as *Chaos* to *G_d*, to each other and to ourselves. There is no sacrifice, no *qorban*, no *'olah*, no *'asham* that can gain access to this latter Garden for we latter Adams and latter Eves."

Abiathar smiled broadly. Such faith. It struck me that His *G_d* was much larger than mine, far more gracious and far more able to redeem. *Abiathar's* eyes were so unlike *Qayin's* at the *Great Altar*. They were full of life. I imagined that they were the eyes of a grandfather who was giving a precious gift to a grandchild. He continued,

"The entire garden, including our own hearts, is polluted and must be experientially purged of all *Chaos*. This is for all of us, particularly for the two priests who live in such vast and dark *Chaos* today. *G_d* alone can only accomplish this. We can only passively watch."

"*G_d* sees our plight, hears our cries and, as He did with Abraham before Him on this very same mountain— He refuses to take the blood of Isaac but instead provides Himself the lamb. It is indeed life-blood provided by *G_d* that purges Eden and Man of pollution that redeems us, or better rebirths us again from the *Chaos*."

"Our role? We are to passively submit by the same faith that empowered our Father Abraham, and only watch as *G_d* purges the messes that we have created. But then, by faith, when the *High Kohen* speaks the words, "It is finished!" we are to go and prepare for the Great Feast of *Booths*, the great recreation of the banqueting of Eden, stripping ourselves of all of our foolish fig leaves and rejoicing with *G_d* in our midst, all of us, including those who had mistreated us, robbed, dishonored us. Can't we see that this is an authentic 'justice'? But it is something far more than this. For justice knows nothing of a rebirth, only payment. This is far more than even justice can engender."

Amen! This day is truly a holy drama, which recreates in us the ancient working of *G_d* to re-establish a higher humanity in community with Him. But I do want to put more thought into the important issue of justice and resolution.

THE JESIAH SCROLLS

14

The Verdict

***Jesiah's* Journal Entry #14-
The *Tenth of Tishri***

The Elders have just announced the verdict to the *kohanim*. After great deliberation—many hours in the Gate of the Temple, the elders have made their judicial decision with regard to *Qayin*, *Tamarah* and *Hevel*. The following is a copy of the official court decision that I have transcribed with great care and precision.

"Let it be known to all Israel on this Holy day:"

"The *Kohen Qayin* is declared to be guilty of unintentional crimes related to the recent events before the court of Elders. *Qayin* is unrighteous with regard to fellow priest *Hevel*, his wife and family, *Tamarah* and her family, his brothers the *Kohanim* of Israel, the entire community of Israel and of course *G_d* Himself. In addition to offering heartfelt repentance to all aforementioned, he is to immediately bring an appropriate *'asham* to the Temple as a right public confession and appropriate payment for his crimes of adultery, deceit, and unfaithfulness. He is to publicly wed *Tamarah* and make room for her in his house as a wife of honor not dishonor. He is to raise the child of their union as a child of honor, equal honor according to the *Torah* as to his other offspring. It is remembered that the first offspring of repentant King David's adultery and murder was taken by G_d as an *'asham*, but that Solomon was also subsequently born of the same union and was a blessing of G_d to Israel. G_d is a G_d of life not death. There is redemption in His hand. With regard to *Tamarah's* family, *Qayin* is to pay to *Tamarah's* family her full rightful dowry as if she was virtuous, for her family is blameless in this matter. *Qayin* will no longer take up his role as one of the assistants to the *High Kohen*. He will instead take his place in a lesser role, though not for dishonor."

"This is to be done for the *shalom* of all Israel which is greater than individual matters."

"*Tamarah* is declared to be guilty of unintentional crimes related to the recent events before the court of Elders. She is unrighteous with regard to *Hevel*, his family and her own family. In addition to offering heartfelt repentance to all the aforementioned, she too is to bring an *'asham* to the Temple as a public confession and payment for her crimes of adultery, deceit, and unfaithfulness. She is to publicly wed *Qayin* and take her place of honor in his family."

"This is to be done for the *shalom* of all Israel which is greater than individual matters."

"*Tamarah's* family is blameless with regard to the events. They are to return the dowry promised to *Hevel's* family with no shame. *Qayin* must pay them the full dowry for *Tamarah* as if she was a virtuous woman. They are to listen to and fully receive the repentance of *Qayin* and *Tamarah* and embrace them. They must now forgive."

"This is to be done for the *shalom* of all Israel
which is greater than individual matters."

"*Hevel* is righteous in this matter and is now freed from all aspects related to the contract of marriage with *Tamarah*. The dowry paid to *Tamarah's* family as part of the betrothal is to be returned in full. *Qayin* is also to pay to *Hevel* and *Hevel's* family any additional expenses that have been paid related to the betrothal, for they are blameless in this matter. *Hevel* and his family are to receive the repentance of *Qayin* and *Tamarah* and accept it. They must now forgive."

"This is to be done for the *shalom* of all Israel
which is greater than individual matters."

"The *kohanim* are righteous in this matter. They must listen to the heartfelt repentance of *Qayin* and *Tamarah* and accept them. They too must now forgive and re-embrace *Qayin* as brother who was astray but has now returned. *G_d* has provided for him purification on this day. *Qayin* is to be restored to our fellowship once his sins have been purged and removed from our midst by the twin goats on this day. May *G_d* forbid that a spirit of judgment and self-righteousness causes division among the *kohanim* of *G_d* this day in Israel."

"This is to be done for the *shalom* of all Israel
which is greater than individual matters."

"During the Atonement ceremony, *Qayin* and *Hevel* are to stand together at the foot of the Great Stairs along with their families at their respective sides; *Tamarah* and her family as well. They must watch *(yir'eh)* together and together receive the atonement of *G_d* for the evil choices made; each of them and their respective families must do this. They must now accept the atonement provided by *G_d* as perfect and must now forgive."

123

"This is to be done for the *shalom* of all Israel
which is greater than individual matters."

"In five days, during the first setting of the *booths*, *Qayin's* family
is to provide the sacred hospitality of the fellowship meal to both
Hevel's and *Tamarah's* family. This is to be received as hospitality
and fellowship by both *Hevel's* and *Tamarah's* family. They must
forgive and be reconciled. Israel must be one again."

"This is to be done for the *shalom* of all Israel
which is greater than individual matters."

"Let no man alter any of the words of the verdict of this Holy
Session or they will be subject to the curse of the One who watches
over Israel, the One who cares for the widow and orphans, the One
who makes the bent things straight."

"This is to be done for the *shalom* of all Israel
which is greater than individual matters."

"Amen and Amen,"

The Elders of Jerusalem

I say to these, Amen. But I wonder in my secret thoughts,
where does justice happen for *Hevel?*

15

The Great Atonement Ceremony

Jesiah's Journal Entry #15-
The _Tenth of Tishri_

The great day has finally arrived. As I write this recollection of the events of the last six hours, I have set aside for a moment my burning question about what we should feel on this day.

My cohort of musicians gathered along the southern portion of the Great Court that surrounds the Temple. Though it is not a prescribed Holy Convocation, the crowd of onlookers had totally filled the Great Court. So much so that one of our important roles was crowd control. Last year, one man was so distraught and so angry that he went out of control. He raced through the crowds knocking down as many people, including children, as he possibly could. Finally, he was tackled and constrained by the Temple guards and held in shackles in one of the courtroom cells until the day was done and he was released to the elders of his tribe. Gladly, nothing of that sort happened this year.

From our vantage point, we could look up the Great Stairs and through the massive doors that lead into the Outer Court of the

Temple. That area was reserved only for the *High Kohen*, *Azariah* and his immediate entourage on this High Holy Day. *Azariah* must have full reign over the whole space and be free to move so that all is done according to prescription, particularly on this day. *Azariah* was not only the *High Kohen*, but a man whose reputation was spotless among us. He was truly a man who was righteous, fearing G_d and keeping His commandments. He was high in stature with a long face, framed in a bushy long grayish white beard. His waist-length white hair is almost always drawn back behind his head and tied with a length of plain brown leather. But what people mostly notice are his eyes, piercing deep-brown eyes that empower his gaze with both intensity and striking compassion. And so he has received the nickname, *Azariah* the Compassionate.

From my location at the southern base of the Great Steps, I could see *Qayin* at the very front of the steps, his visage worn, looking years older. The blood that covered him from a few days ago was cleaned off, but it seemed to me that it is still the death of the sacrifice that now clung to him, not the life. I remembered silently to myself that *Qayin* was supposed to be the honored assistant of the *High Kohen* this year. But of course, that did not happen. Sin indeed comes with its consequences. I felt sorry for him—a little.

On his left hand side a bit closer to me was *Hevel*. I could also recognize some of *Hevel's* family with him. Per the verdict of the court, they had chosen a prominent place in the very front of the steps that lead into the Temple Gate. From there they would be able to clearly see the altar and the offerings being made on behalf of all Israel. I hoped that, particularly for *Hevel's* sake, that perhaps G_d's *kabod* would enter the Temple again as it did two years ago.

Earlier in the day, *Azariah* had gone out onto the great porch at the top of the stairs to the great cheers and cries of all below. He was wearing the bright white linen garment and modest turban prescribed by law for this day alone. The normal priestly garb was beautiful and colorful, intricately embroidered complete with a full retinue of gold and embroidery set apart for his use. But that outfit was noticeably absent. He stood with only a simple unembroidered linen shirt, shorts, sash and turban. Why? Some have speculated that on this day, the *Kohen* takes on the robes of a humiliated servant, white cotton linen, for only the humble may enter the *Holy Place*. Others suggest that these were the garments of the angels. No one can say for certain.

Then he took a spotless bull for a purification sacrifice for himself and his family. No one is without pollution on this day, no not one. All are 'guilty'. Before anything else happens, *Azariah* publicly recognized that he and his family needed purging from sin and the consequences of sin. For only the fully clean may enter Eden, may enter the Holy of Holies and appropriate reconciliation between *G_d* and man.

Azariah brought the bull to the altar, laid his hands on its head and confessed aloud his sins and those of the other *kohanim*.

"I beseech You, O Adonai
I have sinned, rebelled and transgressed against You,
I and my household
And the Sons of Aaron, Your holy people;
I beseech You, O Adonai,
Grant purging for the sins,
And for the iniquities and transgressions
Which I have committed against You,
I and my household
And the Sons of Aaron, Your holy people;
As it is written in the Torah of Your servant Moses;
For on this day atonement shall be made for you,
To purify you from all your sins—
Before the Lord you shall be purified."[xxiii]

And in unison the throngs of thousands responded in like manner, many prostrated themselves to the ground, making no small disruption as the crowd was indeed shoulder-to-shoulder.

"Blessed be the Name of His glorious Kingdom, for ever and ever."

THE JESIAH SCROLLS

This refrain of the masses was repeated time and time again, until the *Azariah* felt it was appropriate to move the ritual forward. This day is not about rote religious repetition and dry ritual. May *G_d* forbid. This day is all about real healing *lipne Elohim*. *Azariah* was acting more like a compassionate physician than an employed Temple minister.

This day, I thought, was particularly filled with poignancy, knowing the crimes of passion within the priesthood. I wondered what *Qayin* was thinking during that prayer? What he must have felt? Or for that matter, *Hevel*. Betrayal is a deep cut. So much was taken from him.

Then *Azariah* slaughtered the bull at the base of the altar, gathering the blood into the golden vessel called the *mizrak* that he passed on to one of his attendants whose sole role was to slowly swirl the contents of the *mizrak* so that it did not congeal. *Azariah* then walked up the ramp of the *Great Altar* in the Outer Court and collected some of the burning coals from the altar fire with the incense shovel. With that in his right hand and one of the Temple's magnificent golden spoons filled with finely ground aromatic incense, carefully prepared to very exact specifications in his left hand, he entered the tall gate that took him out of our sight into the Holy Sanctuary. There he would walk past the Altar of Incense, the Table of the Showbread and the golden candelabras, climb the final ten steep stairs and carefully walk through the veiled opening in the thick wall before him into the awesome High Place, the Holy of Holies.

This happens only once a year, only then by the *High Kohen* and only for this purpose. If he had raised his gaze, there before him would be the two golden *Cherubim*, 15 feet high— their extended wings filling up the 33 foot width of the room. Beneath them, under their gaze is the Holy *Ark of the Covenant*, four and a half feet long, two and a half feet wide, and two and a half feet high.

But the *High Kohen* knows better than to look at the sight, for it is not for unclean polluted man to see *G_d* who dwells between the *Cherubim* on the golden cover of the *Ark*. When we speak of *G_d* dwelling here, we of course do not mean that this is *G_d's* abode, as a man dwells in a framed house. May G_d forbid. There is no palace conceivable to man that is capable of containing *Adonai*. No, it is better understood that this is the official *lipne Elohim*. It is here that the Judge of all the Celestials, the King of the Ages maintains His highest court beyond which there is no appeal. It is here that He does all of His official business with the creation. It is very appropriate to see the business of this specific day as a trial; where everyone, everywhere is the defendant and must face charges laid against them by the Accuser. In this drama, even the *High Kohen* is but a defendant.

So *Azariah* would not dare to gaze upon the face of G_d, rather, he would bow his head and close his eyes in reverence, so as not to look. Do not imagine that he is lost in the darkness. He was well practiced what to do in his charge this day. He would find his way to the place in between the poles that carry the *Ark*. There he would lay the shovel down on the ground and place the double handful of incense on the coals. In a moment, the chamber would become filled with the pungently sweet aromatic smoke. Now he would be able to freely look up without fear of death.

After all of this, still out of the sight of the crowd far below, *Azariah* would have retraced his path out of the Holy of Holies, out to the porch of the Holy place where he would have taken the *mizrak* from the other *Kohen*; entered the Holy sanctuary a second time— to the same place between the carrying poles of the *Ark*; this time amidst choking swirling smoke. Once there, he would have taken some of the bull's blood with his forefinger and sprinkled it once above the east side of the *Ark* cover and seven times before it. By this action, he would have officially purged the pollution caused by His sins and the sins of all the *kohanim* from the *Holy of Holies* and implicitly from the entire Temple.

Once again *Azariah* came into our public view. He walked to the edge of the Great Porch far above us, his formerly pure white linen robe now streaked and splattered with blood. Momentarily, he was enveloped in the rising *'olah*-like cries of the people who were wedged into the outer court below; some swirling cries of great fear, some sorrow, others proclaimed G_d's mercy, some praised *G_d* for His longsuffering and patience with sinners, others cried out angrily for justice. Many voices were too beat up to rise very high in their throats and like *Qayin* yesterday just remained prostrate with mute tongues.

But the *High Kohen* was not done. The Temple was still polluted by the many sins committed by the myriads of people over the last twelve months. *Azariah* quickly moved to begin this next series of purification and purging.

We watched as two magnificent goats were brought to him. They had been chosen from the many brought by the people for this purpose. They were to be virtual twins, spotless charcoal-black Syrian longhaired goats; mature, and male. They were placed before him even as the people below were before him. An assistant brought an urn to *Azariah*. He reached into the urn with both hands and took one of the inscribed lots in each. He held up his right hand over the head of the goat on his right and read aloud the inscription on the lot, "For *Azazel*!" A roar erupted from the crowd. He did not wait for the noise to subside, and held up his left hand with the remaining lot over the head of the other goat and proclaimed in his most priestly voice, "For the Lord!"

His attendants then took of the goat ascribed "For *Azazel*" and tied a red ribbon to its horn. This is the 'Alive-Goat'. But this ceremony must wait for the moment.

Then *Azariah* sacrificed the goat designated 'for the Lord' on the *Great Altar* in the prescribed manner and entered the *Holy of Holies* a third time, this time with a second *mizrak* filled with the blood of the sacrificed goat. Once there in the designated place between the poles of the *Ark*, he would have sprinkled the blood in the exact same manner as the blood of the Bull. Once that was done, it is written that the *High Kohen* through the means of the blood had made atonement for the Most *Holy Place* because of the uncleanness and rebellion of the Israelites, whatever our sins have been. The vile stench of our individual and corporate sin would have been removed from the very nostrils of *G_d*.[xxiv]

Azariah then purified the inner court of the Temple with the combined blood of the bull and goat by sprinkling them on the

Altar of incense in the prescribed manner. Thus through the blood, he cleansed the inner court as well.

Once again, this was out of our direct sight. We who have gathered below could only passively watch and wait for these things to happen. Most of the day's events happen far out of our sight and hearing. We only knew that they occurred when we finally could see *Azariah*, at last, arise to the very top of the *Great Altar* with a single *mizrak* made up of the combined blood of the bull and goat and watched as he cleansed the unseen gross pollution off the *Great Altar* itself by putting some of the combined blood on each of the horns at the corners and then ritually sprinkled the altar in the matter prescribed by Law. It was, as always a powerful and moving experience for us, we descendents of slaves. It is written that by this act, through the purging blood <u>all</u> of the uncleanness of the Israelites was removed from the *Great Altar*, and implicitly the entire Outer Court of the Temple.

But the annual ceremony was still not yet complete. There remained the ceremony of the Alive-Goat that was still being held on the porch of the Temple Outer Court. *Azariah*, now deeply stained by the blood of the purgation offerings stood in front of the Alive-Goat, placed both hands on the animal's head, between its horns, and confessed the sins of the entire people of Israel. Through this mysterious ritual he legally— and mysteriously— put all the sins, including all of the pollution of the sin that was purged off the walls, the floor, the vessels, the altars of the Temple, upon the head of the Alive-Goat.

> *"I beseech You, O Adonai*
> *Grant atonement for the sins,*
> *And for the iniquities and transgressions*
> *Which the entire house of Israel*
> *Has committed against You,*
> *As it is written in the Torah of Your servant Moses;*
> *For on this day atonement shall be made for you,*
> *To purify you from all your sins—*
> *Before the Lord you shall be purified."*[xxv]

131

The entire crowd cried out in a unified response,
"Blessed be the Name of His glorious Kingdom, for ever and ever."

Just after this prayer, the *High Kohen* gave a homily to the gathered, appropriate to the day and time. *Azariah* stood, solemn and glorious, in his white linen streaked with blood and said with a voice of both resonating compassion and fatherly firmness as well:

"We have all, each of us come up to this place, *lipne Elohim* to *yir'eh*, (to see). We each come with burdens, great burdens on our souls that we were <u>not</u> meant to carry. These burdens are made up of two types. First, the overage of *kabod* (glory) that we have wrongly stolen from others or secondly, the absence of the *kabod* that others have robbed from us. Each are great oppressive burdens to man, whether a bounty not due us, or the lack of the bounty that was rightfully ours."

"But it is here, on this day, in this place, *lipne Elohim*, that we are made again to see that the size of these afflictions, our burdens, its mass and weight is a matter of relative perspective. From our perspectives, they are indomitably great; but from the perspective of *Adonai*, they are quite small. By 'great' and 'small', I do not speak of the reality of the size. The Scrolls proclaim that all crimes, even the smallest of crimes, is so great that it is beyond measure. It would be reasonable for us to say in one important sense that we regularly underestimate the size of the crimes and consequences of all crimes made against us. This is a mercy of *G_d*, for if we knew how much *kabod* was really taken from us, or how much *kabod* we took from another, we could not bear it. No, by 'great' and 'small', I am referring to its relative size compared to the *kabod* of the One who truly *yir'ehs*, who truly sees. We, sons and daughters of Adam, east of Eden have had so much of our derivative *kabod* robbed by so many, that our souls are quite destitute and languishing as the wilderness is today with the lack of the seasonal rains which have overlooked us for many months. We are such empty cups.

Forsaken, forsaken! But *Adonai* has no such lack. His *kabod*, unlike ours, is far beyond any measures, eternal, larger than large itself. From His perspective, what we see as great losses of *kabod*, are quite miniscule really. Notice how simply all of the losses and robberies of *kabod* of all Israel are all put on the head of this single goat."

"Oppressed ones, Hear me. Behold! The choice before you today is not to give up justice. May G_d forbid. In fact, it can be rightly said that to carry the burden one second longer than need be is equivalent to choosing to give up justice. For look around you, in this court *lipne Elohim*, justice has already been done. It is far greater than man can *yir'eh*.

Justice, too, is a matter of perspective. Consider how many of your souls cry out for justice, driving you to obsess with getting justice, even if it is the last thing that you do, no matter who in your family, tribe or people gets harmed in the process. Consider in your heart, if it is really 'justice' that you seek; or rather are you yearning for a more personal vindication, a venting of anger and rage instead? People of Israel, Behold! Justice has been done for you. *Yir'eh*, G_d Himself has provided for you a substitute offering just as He promised to Abraham. The trial that you longed for is now complete. The verdict is perfect. 'Guilty' has been proclaimed over all crimes, each and everyone, objective perfect verdict for all crimes against you and by you."

"Behold! Victims, if you indeed were righteous and only wanted justice for the crime that was committed against you, then you are now satisfied. It is finished. Amen? You are truly freed from the enslavement of your sorrow and hurt.

But behold! Is your burden still upon you? Are you still oppressed by the past crimes put upon you by your oppressor? Then you must see that you have refused the resolution and consolation that G_d has dearly provided for you from His endless mercies this day. Can you see that it is no longer the perpetrator who oppresses you? Nor is it the crime that oppresses you, Dear one? No, it is you who oppresses yourself! That is an even greater, more destructive crime. Some of the greatest oppressions are done by victims in response to the victimizations from oppressors. The victim can hold their perpetrator and the community that surrounds them ransom for long periods of time. As one of our sages has rightly said, "The demands of the oppressed and the self-imprisoned that they should be allowed to blackmail the celestials: that until they consent to receive joy (on their own terms) no one else should experience joy; that theirs should be the final power; that *Sheol* should be able to veto Heaven itself."xxvi

"You who have carried your burdens this day up the many steps and risers to come to the heights of the *Holy Place lipne Elohim*, as the smoke of an *'olah* to the very nostril of *G_d's* face, would you now refuse *G_d* the permission to take your burdens off of you? Would you prefer to carry them home with you? If you do, they will be an even greater burden, or better a vile stench, like the public filth, human refuse and garbage that flows down from the high terraces where you now stand, down the swales of the *Central Valley* to the *Valley of Hinnom*, finally there to be cast out of the Holy City to be burned. Would you carry your precious burden there amidst the wailing and gnashing of teeth in your self-made self-pity and affliction?"

"It is said that every disease that submits to a cure will be cured, and vice versa, every disease that will not submit to a cure will never be cured. Amen? All of the sorrows of this place, all of the loneliness, all of the betrayals and heartbreaks, the robberies, the anger, hurt, hatred and envies, and yes, shame and guilt, if they could be rolled into a single experience and placed on a scale against the very slightest of joys that is felt by the very least of all in the eternal realm of *Adonai*, it would measure no weight, none that could be discerned by the most discerning of bankers and money changers. If this ball of the deep sorrow of all gathered here today, nay, all Israel… nay, all the nations were gathered and poured into the vast Great Waters of Heaven's joy and *kabod*, it would be as but a single tiny drop and would bring no noticeable discoloration."

"Victim, you must now choose as the Alive-Goat stands before you, all of you who have had your *kabod* robbed from you this year. You must by faith choose to place your emptiness upon the head of the goat, to let it go, to no longer make it a matter of contention with you. Then watch passively and helplessly as your loss, your emptiness goes away to *Azazel*, never to be seen or measured by your soul again. The G_d who watches over you, who neither slumbers nor sleeps has far more *kabod* than you ever need and freely gives it to those that He elects."

"Likewise, Guilty-one, your choice, all of you who have robbed the *kabod* of others, with foresight, or in ignorance, and now carry the sorrow, the guilt and shame of the act; you too must by faith choose to place your guilt and shame on the head of this goat. The G_d who watches over your victim also watches over you. He alone can restore what you have taken. He can *bara'* into any *Chaos* that has been created by your choices and your acts of evil and ignorance. Watch as all of the pollution and *Chaos* goes to the place where no power on heaven or on earth can return. This does not mean that you can now leave this place and shirk your duty to repent, to pay back what you took according to the Elder's verdicts. Do not shirk the pursuit of reconciliation with the families and individuals involved, for in this is righteousness. Remember that the *Shalom* of Israel is greater than individual issues. So choose to carry your burden no longer. For that would be unbelief of the highest magnitude. Amen and Amen."

Azariah then handed the rope tied to the Alive-Goat to a man who had been designated for this assignment. The latter led the goat, and with it, all of the sins and pollution of Israel purged by G_d Himself on their behalf into the depths of the wilderness and set him loose there, never to return.

I should add here that I am aware of a great deal of discussion about the name *Azazel*. I personally have no problem understanding this *Azazel* to be the same fallen angel of that name from common mythology and folklore. Not to say that I believe or don't believe that there is really a fallen angel of that name. For me, that is not the point. The goat is not to be seen as a ransom to such an entity, or a sacrifice either. None of those would be kosher. It seems preferable that once again, G_d as the great Storyteller is incarnating the crude husks of the world to tell His redemption story.

135

To send the— Alive-Goat to the place of *Azazel* is the same as saying that it is to be sent to the farthest of far away places from which even fallen angels cannot return. The bottom-line is that it will never be seen again.

When *Azariah* was assured that the Alive-Goat was 'to *Azazel*', he re-entered the Inner Court, bathed, adorned himself with the normal priestly garments and then made his final grand appearance for the day, this time in full *High Kohen* regalia, shining white, gold and multiple colors. It was finally time for the great *'olah* sacrifices on behalf of himself and all of the people of Israel. It is written:

"And this shall be to you a law for all time: In the seventh month, on the tenth day of the month, you shall practice self-denial; and you shall do no manner of work, neither the citizen nor the alien who resides among you. For on this day atonement shall be made for you to cleanse you of all your sins; you shall be clean before the LORD."[xxvii]

Then after these things, the stunning *Kohanim Choir* which had taken their place below the *High Kohen* on the steps going up to the Great Porch sang one of the best known of the Songs of *'olah*.[xxviii]

I rejoiced when they said to me,
'We are going to the House of the LORD.'

Our feet stood inside your gates, O Jerusalem,
Jerusalem built up, a city knit together,

To which tribes would make pilgrimage,
The tribes of the LORD, —

As was enjoined upon Israel —
To praise the name of the LORD.

There the thrones of judgment stood,
Thrones of the house of David.

Pray for the well-being of Jerusalem;

May those who love you be at peace.

May there be well-being within your ramparts,
Peace in your citadels.

For the sake of my kin and friends,
I pray for your well-being;

For the sake of the house of the LORD our G_d,
I seek your good.

Then the most amazing series of events happened. Truly it was one of those rare wonderful displays of great alien miracle and power. In some ways it was just as it was two years ago when the *kabod* of *G_d* powerfully came into our midst. But this expression of *G_d's shekinah* was unique. No one bowed to the ground, as we all did last time and cried out *"Adonai* is good and His love endures forever." But we felt the presence of *G_d* nevertheless. The feeling is hard to explain, but I think that the evidence, the fruit if you will, is easy to describe.

In the middle of the crowd at the forefront of the steps, I could see *Qayin* prostrate on the ground once again, but this time there was something different. There, compassionately leaning over *Qayin* was my friend *Hevel.* He, too, was crying, but not in despair. His eyes were lifted toward the sky as he uttered something that I could not discern. But then he looked beneath him at the prostrate body laid before him at the foot of the Temple steps and said,

"I forgive you *Qayin,* for I have seen *(yir'eh)* your sins against me, *Tamarah,* our families, our tribe carried on the head of a goat. Behold! I can see *(yir'eh)* them no longer. This day, *G_d* Himself has provided *(yir'eh)* Himself the lamb, and the pollution caused by your sins are taken on the head of the Alive-Goat to the wilderness of *Azazel. G_d* has re-birthed us as His people this day. We are the same you and I, *lipne Elohim.* Let *Chaos* disrupt no more. Come arise, we must prepare for *booths.*"

137

Then *Hevel* laughed out loud. It was a resonating laugh from deep in his belly. *G_d* had powerfully touched *Hevel*.

"*Qayin*, this day, it is <u>I</u>, *Hevel*, who am <u>my</u> brother's keeper. The heavens must be dancing at such a joke. It is indeed finished. Amen."

It strikes me now, as I pen this journal, considering the events of the day, that what we witnessed moving through the people gathered in the court was a wave, a Spirit wave. It was not the pounding wave of the primordial *Chaos*, rather a gentle, stirring life-giving wave.

Qayin slowly rose to his feet, all the time gazing into *Hevel's* eyes, maybe to see if what *Hevel* said to him could be true. After a pregnant pause, they embraced for the longest of time. All *Qayin* could say was that he was truly sorry for his evil and destructive choices, all of the dishonor that he had brought to *Hevel*, to *Tamarah*, to the families and to the *kohanim* and Temple. *Hevel* responded only with a firm embrace of great honor, I thought. That wave of honor spread as *Hevel's* family obviously moved by *Hevel's* actions also reached out and began to embrace *Qayin's* family—and *Tamarah's*. It was a powerful moment. Someone, I now wonder if it was *Tamarah*, because her voice is much richer than one would expect from her age, started singing, much like Miriam did so long ago. She sang about Israel's oneness as a people, about *G_d's* faithfulness. A circle was formed of Israelites dancing and singing around the two men and woman. The circle grew into a larger one as one by one other people were caught up into the dance; its encircling arms reaching total strangers. Who could resist such a celebration in Israel.

I am not making this up. At that very moment, rain began to fall as if choreographed by a celestial choir director. In fact, the rain began to fall in great earnest. We know of rains such as this, but usually, almost always in the month of *Chislev* or *Tebeth*, or perhaps as late as in *Shebat*. But this year, such a rain—and in *Tishri*! Long before the time even for early rains.

As the rains continued to pour down, the many stone cisterns designed to catch fresh runoff began to overflow. Sheets of water cascaded off the hard limestone floor and rolled down the great steps of the Temple and courtyard. As they did, each successive step became red, as the blood of the many sacrifices washed down closer and closer to the Great Court and the people below. No one seemed to mind. The dancing continued, circles were forming, voices raised in praise, hands extended upward as *'olah*s. G_d has provided once again for us in ways that are spectacular and mysterious.

What are we to feel as we come to these days? Indeed!

THE JESIAH SCROLLS

16

Where is Justice After All?

Jesiah's Journal Entry #16-
The Eleventh of *Tishri*

Yesterday, the waves of *Chaos* knew defeat again. As the Coronation Hymns proclaimed, the floods of *Chaos* had lifted themselves up against *Adonai* and were soundly defeated. *Adonai* remains on His great throne unchallenged. His statutes are unmovable and trustworthy.

> *Sing to Adonai a new song for He has done unimaginable things*
> *It is His right hand and His holy arm*
> *That have made liberation on His own behalf*
> *The Lord has made His salvation known and*
> *Revealed to the eyes of the goyim His righteousness.*
> *He has remembered His covenant promises and*
> *His faithfulness to the house of Israel;*
> *All the ends of the earth have seen the salvation of our G_d.* [xxix]

Israel was created afresh yesterday. There was a new Exodus for *G_d's* people. The new slaves born from slaves from other slaves before them tasted freedom once more; another external redemption from our sins. We did nothing to accomplish this or to earn this. It was *Adonai* Himself who made it possible. He spoke order once again into the *Chaos* as we watched as helpless failures.

He, for just a moment in time has re-created Eden, a place where He can freely dwell among His people. We, His people by faith were recreated as well; the pollution and *Chaos* in our souls and lives were purged. We were re-birthed and could now by faith re-enter Eden.

It was a powerful thing to see the Alive-Goat led into the wilderness and to deeply meditate on the ramifications of purging accomplished by *G_d* alone. Then to hear the *High Kohen*, speaking on behalf of *G_d* say, "You are now clean from all your sins!" That was a stunning moment. At the end of the events, the *High Kohen* put back on his normal priestly garb and made an *'olah* for himself and for all Israel. The Temple had been purified by a heavenly detergent— purged of all pollution. There was now nothing hindering our fellowship with *G_d* and with each other, *lipne Elohim*. Justice fully and completely satisfied; our many crimes fully paid for by substitution.

The *High Kohen* raised his arms to the sky and proclaimed, "It is finished." *G_d* is favorable to Israel again. We were dismissed. Now at last, in spite of everything that had happened in recent days and weeks, we were indeed ready to dance at *Sukkoth*, for *G_d* has Himself provided a lamb for His people. It was a miracle.

So, what then is justice? *Hevel* would be so proud of me that I would ask such a philosophical question. Here are my current clumsy thoughts.

For the <u>victim</u>, perfect justice must offer true and lasting vindication, a proper day in court:

> where they can make the public case of the crime perpetrated upon them,
>
> where before a proper, objective compassionate Judge, they can tell their story,

where the guilty can be publicly condemned,

where there would be a public, trustworthy assurance of real restoration of what was taken, and a public trustworthy assurance that the perpetrator will be appropriately punished (no more, no less), and of course

where an actual restoration of the *shalom* that was before the crime.

Amen? For the victim, this is justice. It strikes me that all of these are integral to the machinations of the *High Holy Days* of Israel. These things can only occur on these days *lipne Elohim*. These things require the High Judge's intimate presence and workings. *Hevel* would say that he had experienced a new *shalom*. It was different than it was before, but no less. He experienced the glory of G_d toward him—the G_d who is no stranger to speaking into *Chaos* and creating substance. Though the loss of *Tamarah* and the loss of so much else due to *Qayin's* betrayal were real and very deep for my friend, he would say that there has been a mysterious wonderful restoration. What is gone is gone, but now there is something new. Mourning the loss was important—but now it is time to celebrate the gain.

For the perpetrator, perfect justice must be fully engaged as well. They too must have their day in court:

where before an objective compassionate Judge who loves them, they can make a public case for all of the crimes committed by them and against them,

where they too can tell their story,

where they can hear an objective verdict and proclamation of their real guilt (as opposed to all of the destructive lying guilt)

where they can be assured that the Judge Himself can actually restore what he, the perpetrator took and lastly

where they can begin to have a great hope that G_d Himself is invested in re-creating *Shalom*.

Amen? For the perpetrator, this is justice. It strikes me that all of these are integral to the machinations of the *High Holy Days* of Israel. These things can only occur on these days, *lipne Elohim*. *Qayin* too has experienced a justice with *shalom*. There are consequences humanly speaking, many in fact. There is nothing he could humanly do to pay back what was taken, or detergent enough to clean what his hands had defiled. So *G_d* comes alongside and stands in for the supplicant and offers a better more sufficient offering. *Qayin's* sacrifice was totally insufficient, not just the pathetic one that he eventually brought to the Temple in his shame, but even the one that bore *Yir'eh*. So *G_d* intervened on his behalf. What an amazing *G_d* Israel serves!

These days are about reconciliation. This can only happen in the powerful covenantal presence of *G_d*. Here *G_d* can *bara'* new life in the worst of *Chaos*.

Amen and Amen!

17

The 70 Bulls of *Sukkoth*

***Jesiah's* Journal Entry #17**

Though the evenings are filled with dancing, singing, eating and other revelries, the days are overwhelmingly busy for the Temple and its servants. We must remain in excellent physical condition, for the rigors of the job are quite demanding. There is no time on the calendar where more demands are put on the Temple than this eight-day period. In addition to regular offerings of the day on behalf of Israel, and the myriad of special offerings—mainly guilt offerings brought by the myriad of pilgrims, we also are commanded by G_d to make a grand sacrifice on the behalf of the other nations.

On each day multiple bulls, rams and goats are offered as *'olah*s on the *Great Altar*. On the first day in particular 13 prime young virile bulls are offered to G_d on behalf of the other nations in absentia. In total throughout the week, 70 bulls, representing the 70 other nations are offered to *G_d* on their behalf. Then each day, a goat is also presented on their behalf as a purification offering to cleanse the Temple from their sins as well.

Why do we do this? Many of these nations are actual enemies of Israel. The elders teach that there are five reasons. First, during this great festival, the nations are actually present in Jerusalem. The city has visitors from all 70 nations, no doubt. I myself have seen caravans from the East, *Babylon* I assumed, ambassadors from Egypt and of course *Sheba* and a number of visitors from places which I have never heard of before. There was one rumor that I heard from a friend that one of the caravans from the southern regions was dramatically interrupted when one of the *wadis* near *En-Gedi* overflowed sweeping four or five unsuspecting camels into the Salt Sea. Fortunately no people perished in the flood. Certainly, the joyous reputation of the Great Feast has spread throughout the world. The nations have come to Israel to celebrate our festival with us. Perhaps *Elohim* is accommodating their ignorance by providing a ram for them as well on this day?

Secondly, these seventy bulls remind us that we too were of the nations when *G_d* found us. Abraham was elected from the bowels of the nations of the east, Ur of the Chaldeans. We are reminded that we are no different from the seventy nations except that *G_d* extended His hand to us as His *segullah*.

Third, it is on these celebratory days that we remember that *G_d's* heart is also for the nations. We are all equally descendants of Adam and Eve. Did not *G_d* tell our father Abraham in the *Torah* that he would be the father of many nations?[xxx] Did not *G_d* also show glory and covenant mercies to the ancient *Qayin* as well as to his brother *Hevel*, to Esau as well as to Jacob, to Ishmael as well as to Isaac? *G_d* has raised Israel up in these last days, not merely to be a receptacle of His blessings alone, but to be a blessing to the nations— a light to the world of *G_d's* name and reign.

Fourth, it is on these celebratory days that the Temple must be purged from <u>all</u> sins of <u>all</u> mankind, not just Israel. G_d is Lord Judge over all the earth. This is His only throne.

Fifth, it is to serve as an invitation and a warning. As we sing in one of our psalms,[xxxi]

"Why do nations assemble, and peoples plot vain things;
Kings of the earth take their stand, and
Regents intrigue together against the LORD and against His anointed?
'Let us break the cords of their yoke,
shake off their ropes from us!'
He who is enthroned in heaven laughs;
The Lord mocks at them.
Then He speaks to them in anger,
Terrifying them in His rage,
'But I have installed My king on Zion, My holy mountain!'
Let me tell of the decree: the LORD said to me,

'You are My son,
I have fathered you this day.
Ask it of Me, and I will make
The nations— Your domain;
Your estate— the limits of the earth.
You can smash them with an iron mace,
Shatter them like potter's ware.'

So now, O kings— be prudent;
Accept discipline— you rulers of the earth!
Serve the LORD in awe;
Tremble with fright,
Pay homage in good faith,
Lest He be angered, and
Your way be doomed in the mere flash of His anger.
Happy are all who take refuge in Him."

The rebellious nations are called to come to G_d's ordained Son on earth and proclaim their allegiance. This is not a negative thing at all. The anointed King offers the power of reconciliation and life to all who come and bow. This we have seen and

147

experienced. Just yesterday. Only the hard-hearted, the arrogant or the deceived would choose not to come.

Israel's role is mysterious and glorious, far beyond any calling that we would be innately worthy of. We were birthed out of the same flesh as the other nations. But *Adonai* invites the nations to come to Jerusalem to enter His covenant—the single covenant made with Adam, with Noah, with Abraham and with the Great King David.

I am reminded of when, only two years ago, on the very eve of the fifteenth of *Tishri*, during the seventh year of debt forgiveness, the stunning sight of King Solomon's ordination being renewed in the court of the Temple on a special platform built for the occasion. He was dressed in simple clothes, simple linen garments befitting a servant versus a King of his stature. On that dais, in front of representatives from all Israel and ambassadors from many nations who had come to witness this event (and of course the Great Feast as well only a couple of days afterwards), the *High Kohen* laid his hands upon the exposed naked head of the King and sang this Psalm over him.

"You are my Son; today I have become your Father. Ask of me, and I will make the nations your inheritance, the ends of the earth your possession. You will rule them with an iron scepter; you will dash them to pieces like pottery…!"

At this point in the reading, the King rose, head still bowed as an act of submission *lipne Elohim*, and the crown of his father replaced on his head, a kingly golden robe draped over his shoulders.

He rose as the King of Israel, the Anointed One, the Son of G_d.

Then the *High Kohen* spoke to the witnesses, representatives no doubt of all of the 70 nations scattered throughout the globe, representing all of the seed of Adam and Eve, and made a bold invitation, with his back facing the *Holy Place*, speaking as if *G_d* were speaking to his scattered people east of Eden,

"Therefore, you kings, be wise; be warned, you rulers of the earth. Serve the LORD with fear and rejoice with trembling. Kiss

148

the Son, lest he be angry and you be destroyed in your way, for his wrath can flare up in a moment. Blessed are all who take refuge in him."[xxxii]

This caused no little commotion among the gentile ambassadors as you can imagine!

It is ironic to me that though gentile ambassadors come from all of the 70 nations with their own agendas and plans, this day we are the ambassadors of *Adonai* to them. On this day, there is a promise to them and a warning. There is unbelievable joy and life and refuge under His *Sukkoth*—and there is judgment and destruction for all not under His protection and favor.

THE JESIAH SCROLLS

18

Temporary *Booths* and Hospitality

***Jesiah's* Journal Entry #18**

The few times that I dared to travel from the Temple courts in the last two days, I could hardly make my way through the crowded streets of Jerusalem. Spirits are very high and preparations for the great Festival are close to being finalized. The prophet Moses commanded all Israel to come to Jerusalem for the great annual fall festival and live in *booths* crudely made out of a variety of boughs from majestic trees, such as palm branches, long stems of the river willows, and other leafy branches. And so virtually overnight, the city expands from being contained within its fortified walls to a sprawling green city that spreads in rows and rows into the valleys of *Kidron*, *Hinnom* and up the sides of the hills around us. Everywhere one looks is a forest of green boughs, filled with movement, activity, cooking, celebrating and of course, the songs of pilgrims, the going-up songs. One of the favorites of the pilgrims...I have heard it sung in at least three languages ... maybe more this very year— is the *Samachti, the 'rejoicing'*,

"I rejoiced when they said to me,
'We are going to the House of the LORD.'
Our feet stood inside your gates, O Jerusalem,

Jerusalem built up, a city knit together,
To which tribes would make pilgrimage,
The tribes of the LORD,
As was enjoined upon Israel
To praise the name of the LORD.

There the thrones of judgment stood,
Thrones of the house of David.

Pray for the well-being of Jerusalem;
May those who love you be at peace.
May there be well-being within your ramparts,
*Peace in your citadels."*xxxiii

What are the *booths* to teach us? Once again Israel is a nomad people, remembering what it was like when our forefathers and mothers were set free from Egypt and were reconciled with *G_d*. The words of *Hevel* were right when he suggested that our forbearers were not comfortable with the grace offered by *G_d*. But I also suspect that as slaves they were equally uncomfortable with living in *booths* in the wilderness, unable to do anything to further their own survival. They were to learn how to trust their lives to *G_d*, to passively receive from *G_d* alone what they did not deserve and could not earn by their own efforts or control.

But there is another reason that we dwell in *booths*. Not only do we remember *G_d's* provision for us but we remember our charge to extend it to others. Righteousness demands that we extend hospitality to everyone on this day. No one goes hungry. Everyone is a special honored guest at some table in Jerusalem. This is true this week whether one is a servant, a sojourner, or a visitor. Everybody enjoys the righteousness of *Adonai* through the means of His people's graciousness and hospitality.

I said to my heart, this is especially wonderful in the case of painful relational breaches in the community such as the recent conflict between *Qayin* and *Hevel*. Today, the Elders commanded that the three families involved eat a fellowship meal together to publicly signify that the conflict is over between them. What had been dishonor, through the means of the purging on the *Day of Atonement*, has been made to be honor for them. There is another one of the going-up songs of the pilgrims written by King David himself,[xxxiv]

> *How good and how pleasant it is that brothers dwell together.*
> *It is like fine oil on the head*
> *Running down onto the beard,*
> *The beard of Aaron,*
> *That comes down over the collar of his robe;*
> *Like the dew of Hermon*
> *That falls upon the mountains of Zion.*
> *There the LORD ordained blessing,*
> *Everlasting life.*

The Lord has done great things for us—indeed.

THE JESIAH SCROLLS

19

The Party

Journal entry #19-
The *Fourteenth of Tishri*

The generous storm of a couple of days ago has already become a thing of some legend. The rain itself was quickly absorbed into the dusty limestone soil; no more was to be seen. The few puddles that had collected on the streets of the city have quickly dried up in the hot *Tishri* sun. Yet everybody is still talking about the mysterious freak storm. It is said that good news travels almost as fast as bad news in Israel. It is so in this case. People who were not even present, but heard about it second hand, are spreading the story to others who have come for the festival.

Truly in our land, and in particular in this time, after the final harvests of the year, the thoughts of all turn to the next year. Would the drought finally end? Some say that Israel has been in drought for two years; others argue that it began five years ago. But all would agree that we need rain, and all agree that no one has the power to make it so other than *Adonai* Himself.

We *kohanim* have noted the dramatic increase in the number of offerings that have been made *lipne Elohim* requesting rain for Israel. Extraordinary preparations were made to accommodate an even larger crowd for today's seventh day *Hosheana* ritual in the Temple Outer Court. Today, the court was packed with supplicants from all over the 70 nations, each with palm and long willow branches or other greenery in their hands waving them in unison as the responsive litany begins.[xxxv]

First the *kohanim* sang, and the people responded each time with a bold glorious "his love endures forever!"

> *Give thanks to Adonai, for he is good;*
> > *His love endures forever.*
> *Let Israel say:*
> > *"His love endures forever."*
> *Let the house of Aaron say:*
> > *"His love endures forever."*
> *Let the pious who fear Adonai say:*
> > *"His love endures forever."*

After repeating the section a number of times, one of the senior *kohen* cantors began to sing in a haunting melodic tune,

> *I was being crushed in my constraints*
> *But I cried out to Yah*
> *He responded by placing me on a wide place.*

I thought to myself that much of the crushing this year was coming from the heat of the Sun itself. We cry out to G_d for relief. The cantor continued as people settled themselves to listen. They waited ever so impatiently for the grand culmination of the song. I noticed some jockeying for position closest to the altar, perhaps thinking that G_d's attention is limited by a few feet?

> *Adonai is with me; I will not be afraid. What can man do to me?*
> *Adonai is with me; he is my helper. I will look in triumph on my enemies.*[xxxvi]

Another choir lifted up their voices to sing a response to the couplet

It is better to take refuge in Adonai than to trust in man.
It is better to take refuge in Adonai than to trust in princes.

The cantor continued with the choir responding

All the nations surrounded me,
But in the name of Adonai I cut them off.
They surrounded me on every side,
But in the name of Adonai I cut them off.
They swarmed around me like bees,
But they died out as quickly as burning thorns;
In the name of the LORD I cut them off.
I was pushed back and about to fall,
But Adonai helped me.

Adonai is my strength and my song; he has become my salvation.
Shouts of joy and victory resound in the tents of the righteous:
"Adonai's right hand has done mighty things!
Adonai's right hand is lifted high;
Adonai's right hand has done mighty things!"

I will not die but live,
And will proclaim what Adonai has done.
Adonai has chastened me severely,
But he has not given me over to death.
Open for me the gates of righteousness;
I will enter and give thanks to Adonai.
This is the gate of Adonai through which the righteous may enter.
I will give you thanks, for you answered me;
You have become my salvation.
The stone the builders rejected has become the capstone;
Adonai has done this, and it is marvelous in our eyes.
This is the day Adonai has made; let us rejoice and be glad in it.

Then the *kohanim* en-masse went around the *Great Altar* with our branches waving, seven times each singing
'Ana' Adonai hoshe'ah n'a
'Ana' Adonai hatsliachah n'a.

Please Adonai, save us now,
Please Adonai, prosper us now!

Meanwhile, the crowd joined in singing to *Adonai* and waving their branches. The scene has been described as a sea of green branches waving like an ocean, ebbs and flows rising up only to pound them to the ground. Some of the voices were joyful, others were crying out in desperation in concert with the words.
'Ana' Adonai hoshe'ah n'a
'Ana' Adonai hatsliachah n'a.

After the circling was completed the choir erupted once again,
"Blessed is he who comes in the name of the LORD.
From the house of the LORD we bless you.
Adonai is G_d, and he has made his light shine upon us.
With boughs in hand,
Join in the festal procession up to the horns of the altar.
You are my G_d, and I will give you thanks;
You are my G_d, and I will exalt you.

Give thanks to Adonai, for he is good;
His love endures forever. "[xxxvii]

After the event, the Great Court was littered with the beaten leaves and branches that were scattered and broken during the event. Last year it took the *kohanim* and servants almost a week to clean up just the courtyard.

Certainly what all pilgrims desired this year was G_d's provision of rain. This year, all hopes are high because G_d had already begun to provide rain out of season. At yesterday's water libation ceremony, the Outer Court was also fully packed with pilgrims who wanted to pray for rain. The *kohen* who took the golden pitcher of water from the Pool of *Siloam* (where *Hevel* and I were a few days before) and poured it upon the *Great Altar*, loudly imploring G_d for much needed rain in Israel and of course for the 70 nations.

Many of our neighbors have a similar ceremony using water to magically empower their gods to cause rain, or as some flippantly say, to remind their gods to turn the celestial well crank. We mean no such thing. This is the ceremony that the Lord commands. In it we recognize that we are helpless and are totally dependant on G_d for rain as our ancestors depended upon G_d for water in the wilderness. Amen?

But the second aspect of the legend forming around this year's downpour is also spreading throughout the rows and rows of *booths* going up throughout the valleys and hills that surround Jerusalem. The heavens opened up upon the people at the very moment when the *High Kohen* proclaimed that our sins had been washed away. Certainly G_d's heavenly water is as much or more needed this year as regular water. There are many kinds of droughts, aren't there? The story of this year's rainfall will be told for generations no doubt.

THE JESIAH SCROLLS

20

Hevel Reprise

***Jesiah's* Journal Entry #20**

I was anxious to hear from *Hevel* how the *Sukkoth* meal went. I would have guessed that it would have been very awkward to eat alongside of *Qayin* and *Tamarah*. It would be awkward for me, I think. I celebrated *Sukkoth* with a couple of dozen other temple musicians. We ate and drank and sang way too much. Believe me, we did not sing a single song of *Heman*. This was a time for celebration and thanksgiving. But *Hevel's Sukkoth* experience was very different. It was a reconciliation meal.

I am told that some of the bedouin tribes in the rural *Negev* have a similar reconciliation ceremony, the *mishloach*. The *mishloach* is normally done on the main street in the familial village of the victim, in as public a place as possible.

The offender's immediate and extended family would line up on the north side of the street facing the victim's family that would line up opposite them on the south side. In the presence of the tribal elders and witnesses, the offender would cross the imaginary central line to come face to face with the victim. He loudly, not inappropriately, but just so everyone in the court could hear, would repent for all of his crimes against him and their deity. Then the perpetrator would go person to person on the victim's family line and would repeat his confession and repentance until none were left.

Now it would be the victim's family's turn to cross over to receive a cup of bitter coffee, another acknowledgement that they had been victimized. It is a heavy ceremony, though very important. At this point, both families would be required to embrace and to reconcile.

In Israel this is accomplished at a table shared by both families, ideally during *Sukkoth*.

Hevel told me just a little while ago that it was quite a scene. He said that the tables were set length-wise in a specially laid out oblong booth. *Hevel* with his two parents and *Qayin* with his current wife sat at a large head table that overlooked the other tables. *Tamarah* was still with her family to *Qayin's* left. Initially, in spite of the wave of glory that had overcome them five days before, this was understandably quite awkward and conversation quite clumsy. Oh how I wish I could have been there.

Then, according to *Hevel*, the legal representative from the Temple, *Abiathar* himself, stood up and re-read the verdict writ. I thought that this choice of elders was a good one. He is known as both a no-nonsense sort of person and also one who has a remarkable sense of humor. His laugh is deep, resonating, and frankly, legendary. He commands a respect from people who come to him for counsel and advice.

He solemnly read the verdict, pausing after each count, emphasizing the importance of the community over the individual. Then, he laid the scroll down and broke out in a smile that rained warmth over all tables. "It is finished," his bass voice declared,

"It is finished! Let it be proclaimed here, that all that was done before, is now finished! Is there any who would argue this point? This is not to say that everything is as it was. That would be the voice of error. Everything is not the same, but here in the shadow of G_d's courtroom, all voices have been heard, all charges recorded, and verdicts proclaimed. It is now finished. What is left then is for us, the two families gathered in this *Sukkoth* to proclaim to the other *booths*, to all Israel, in fact to all of the 70 nations, that we have embraced G_d's reconciliation. This does not mean that there is no need for further reconciliation. There is. Trust takes time and consistent effort. Community must continually be healed. But because of G_d's power and intervention, it is true that today, in this place, Israel is one again."

Then according to *Hevel*, *Abiathar* stopped, looked around the room as if looking into each face; perhaps to make sure of something, maybe looking for something specific in each soul? Then he held up a leg of lamb on the platter before him and said,

"Now, for me, I don't think that I can wait any longer. The cooking skills of the *Qayin* family are legendary and I really must eat. Rejoice Israel, for you are blessed!"

As I write this in my journal, my head is still woozy from too much wine. But honestly, I still do not fully relate to what happened in *Hevel's* soul. I am still angry and sad over his loss. I cannot imagine eating alongside of *Qayin* at a fellowship meal. I know that it is important to G_d that *shalom* reigns over Israel. I understand that. I know that this *shalom* is not the same as trust, or intimacy— those take time and consistency. No doubt *Qayin* has significant work to do in order to be fully restored.

But *Hevel* believes— in spite of what I feel— or in spite of what I think that I feel— that true *shalom* was manifested here today. Nothing faked— nothing done by human hands. I wondered if *Hevel* was merely in denial. *Hevel* himself argued that this would be a common strategy for slaves. *Hevel* merely laughed and hugged me when I brought up that possibility.

He believes that a miracle of G_d has taken place again— something different; something far more glorious than is humanly possible. Prophetic maybe?

163

I wonder if *G_d's* glory did come into the Temple this year? Not into the Holy place as much as into the shredded community of Israel— into the violated priesthood— into the unforgivable tear that separated *Qayin* and *Hevel, Hevel* and *Tamarah, Qayin* and his first wife. I laugh to myself wondering if at last the ancient narrative of *Qayin* and *Hevel* has finally been redeemed? What they could not accomplish, *G_d* has in these latter days perfectly accomplished?

I wonder if such reconciliation is even imagined much less openly spoken of among any other people? No, it must not be so anywhere other than in the shadow of the court of *G_d*. For such a reconciliation to be more than just bluster, political expediency or wishful thinking, there must first be justice. There is only justice *lipne Elohim*.

21

The Prophets In Town

Jesiah's Journal Entry #21

A no small furor arose today in the palace campus. Israel, unlike the other nations around us is not a Kingdom— per se— that is ruled by a single king. Israel functionally runs under the shared authority of three separated powers, each of which sustains their authority underneath the authority of G_d, each specifically chosen and ordained by G_d Himself. They are: the King, the Priesthood and the Prophets. It would seem that G_d knows that unchecked, unbalanced power in the hands of any son of Adam would be disastrous. And so the King, the anointed Son of G_d, is chosen by means of the prophet and so ordained. He is charged to rule G_d's people with wisdom and discernment that can only be gained from G_d. The King cannot usurp the power of the priesthood. It is not done. It would be an offense to G_d. Nor can the Priest usurp the role of the King. That too would be an abomination. Each has their own prescribed authority and role under G_d.

Likewise, the prophet is also chosen and ordained by G_d, most often through the mediatorship of another prophet.

THE JESIAH SCROLLS

The *High Kohen* is also chosen by *G_d*, but must come specifically from the tribe of Zadok. The choices of office are not up to King, Priest or Prophet, but are *G_d's* alone.

Should a King, or for that matter a *High Kohen*, or even the entire nation stray, as we know is possible from the *Bathsheba* affair during the reign of the Great King David himself, the prophet is often quite instrumental in correcting matters. He is a sword in the arm of *G_d* to restore a *shalom* of righteousness and justice. The voices of the prophets have been silent for a number of years, at least here in Jerusalem. But today, the cry of the prophet was again heard resounding, not at the Temple but rather in the royal palace vicinity, "Thus says the Lord, your *G_d*...." Needless to say, when a prophet visits Jerusalem, it gathers a crowd.

Nathan the prophet came to the Holy city today. "Thus says the Lord, your *G_d*, O Israel..."

By the time I got to the palace courtyard, a huge crowd had already surrounded the prophet and his disciples, six or seven of them by my count. They were gathered by a free standing stone cistern which was filled to the very brim with the runoff collected from the surprise rainstorm earlier. Nathan was dressed in bright orange, glowing in the sunshine. He was elderly, but hardly incapacitated. He was fully alert and spry for a man his age. He spoke with a loud, I would say almost harsh voice and tone. He was not mincing any words. There was some urgency, and yet it did not feel like he needed to overstate to make a point. He was the appointed prophet of *G_d*. He was *G-d's* ambassador. He was a man on a mission, who did not need anyone's approval or support. He was not afraid of priest or King—only *Adonai*. As he spoke in the very shadow of the King's palace, his disciples wrote down what he said.

I had missed some of the prophet's comments. By the time I arrived, he was dipping a ladle into the cistern, and scattering the precious water all over the nearby crowd—drenching them. He began to speak again,

"Thus says the Lord. Oh Israel, look at you, drenched in the rain that I have provided in abundance for you once again. You

166

were helpless, at odds with the sun, powerless over the harvest. Could anyone here command the clouds to give forth abundant waters? Could anyone here command the sun to hide behind the clouds? What King here has such authority? Who here has the wisdom to know how the sky works? Who in this place can discern how I establish the clouds, the mechanisms I use to make the thunder roar and the lightning flash? Does anyone in this royal city of my servant David have the wisdom and discernment to grasp the inner workings of the expanse of the earth, the path of the sun, the mysteries of the myriads of stars in the heavenlies? Who among you is the most wise, the most discerning, let him debate with me. Can he tell me when the sky might open up again? Can he teach me where to find water for my people?"

"Are there other gods who can stand up and speak? Go ahead, look to the south. Do you not remember what I did to the great deities of Egypt? Did they provide rain for you? Life for you? Did they cause your crops to grow, your vineyards to flourish and your vats to overflow? Or did they only put strangling chains around you? Did they make you objects for their own pleasure? What did your redemption as my Son accomplish? Didn't I wed you to Me even while the smell of Egypt still dripped over you like the water from this barrel?"

I wonder if the Prophet was making a not-so-veiled reference to the King's marriage to the Egyptian?

"Oh foolish Israel, use good judgment. Oh my foolish Son, show understanding. See Wisdom and how she clings to me, and dances alongside of me as I speak forth into *Chaos* and life and light both take shape. Each day requires a new dawn, a new sunrise, a new night sky. Hear Wisdom continually calling out to you in the courts of Jerusalem, amid the columns of the palace and royal estates. She cannot be treated so lightly or taken for granted, or poorly pursued. Only the foolish lean on gold, or on silver. Only the dull and undiscerning rely on détente and ill-pursued peace treaties with deaf and dumb gods who have no compassion for my Son. What does wisdom have to do with politics; discernment with a policy of appeasement? What does *shalom* have to do with

167

man's perceived plans? Where do the rains of Israel's greatness and calling come from? Is it not written that the King must not gather to himself many horses lest his heart turn away?"xxxviii

As Nathan said this, he looked squarely at the new construction at the Palace, the home for the King's many new wives.

"There is time to hear yet, my wayward Son, for only a little while. There will come a deluge, a destructive flood from the east, flooding the *Yarmuk* from beyond *Gamala*—with a force that can cut through great mountains. O woe to you proud mountain fortress *Gamala*, you too thought that you were infinite, your walls immeasurable, and your heights unassailable. But you will see. A flood is coming upon you, a devastation that would be unimaginable to this generation. There will be no recovery. Pursue wisdom and discernment from *G_d* again."

With those words done, the prophet seemed to age 50 years. His frame, which was erect and straight only moments before— seemingly indefatigable— was now deeply bent over, held up only by two spindly legs and a thin worn cane, all three shaking noticeably. His students quickly came alongside their quivering, now all too human it would seem, master and began the laborious journey to their resting place.

What did his words mean? It remains a great debate in the city. No one seems to be too confident of their interpretation. I have my suspicions of course. Nathan's eyes were telling I think. But I am not a prophet or the son of a prophet. Many wonder if the words were more for our Great King Solomon than anyone else? It is a foolish person who speculates too much about the doings of the royal family. I will shut my mouth. I can say this though, the prophetic visit had clearly put a damper on the royal wedding celebration.

Note to self. I just found out that *Tamarah* has a younger sister who is not yet given to a man. She is twelve years old and therefore very marriageable. The person who mentioned her to me said that she is strong, an excellent cook and has *Tamarah's* eyes and laugh. I do not say this arrogantly, or with too high of a measure of my worth, but I deserve such a bride—but I must move quickly. *Hevel* gave his hearty approval—I was glad about that. May *G_d* smile upon me.

Author's note: *The prophets play only a minor cameo role in Jesiah's story, but they will play much larger roles in some other of Abba's tales yet to come. Selah.*

THE JESIAH SCROLLS

22

Yir'eh! The Final Word

***Jesiah's* Journal Entry #22**

I have now had more time to ponder the events of these Holy days. I see now that I was asking the wrong question. I was curious to know what we as individual Jews and as the people of *G_d* are supposed to feel or experience on these days. But it now seems to me to be a bit of an irrelevant question—maybe imprecise is a better way of describing it. Everything changed for Israel two years ago when the glory of *G_d* entered the *Holy Place*. This year, everything changed for *Hevel* as *G_d's* glory entered again. It is not about what we are to <u>feel</u> but who we are to <u>be</u> *lipne Elohim*. Here on these days, the very order of creation becomes powerfully and experientially restored between *G_d* and man at least for a moment of time. Individuals come fractured and leave whole. But *Adonai* demands more. There is reconciliation here for the irreconcilable. That is an unimaginable gift; great mercy extended to unworthy bickering, abusive and abused slaves by the Great Creator. There is reconciliation for great crimes among us. I think of *Qayin's* great crime of lust. It was indeed very *high handed* at its roots, very destructive, and very thoughtless to all involved. But here in this place, *G_d* has provided a lamb for him, for *Hevel*, for *Tamarah*. Here, real and substantive healing is provided and is accessible to all who would come.

But it is even larger still. On these days the 70 nations are commanded— invited to come and access this reconciliation. Can you imagine? Hittites, Philistines, Ethiopians, Edomites, Israel, the other warring nations of the north and east— reconciled? Sharing together as distinct yet one at a single feast *lipne Elohim*.

Israel comes to this place each year to be reminded again that we are Israel-who-abides-*lipne Elohim*. For twelve months we wander, much like the *Qayin* of old, trying to be Adam-apart-from-*G_d*. But even at our best, we fail year after year. But in the month of *Tishri*, *G_d* prepares our return, provides the means and the purgation on our behalf. We, descendents of slaves, are invited to come and dance at *G_d's* feast as redeemed people of His glory. We are transformed to be dancers. Not only that, we are transformed even deeper to really <u>want</u> to be dancers. This is the miracle of *Sukkoth*.

But not just us. I look around at the miracle of the 70 nations coming together before the Creator *G_d* and get a sense of the abnormality of the event. There was a time and a place before our father and mother's illicit reach of unbelief planted the seeds of what is now a deep, widespread alienation among us. As I write this, I am looking down from one of the highest eastern parapets of the Temple, overlooking the entire stretch of the great *Kidron Valley* while as the *booths* are now being razed to the ground, families gathered, multi-colored, multi-national caravans from the four winds begin to peel out of the valley, to the north, south, east and west. They have come to this place, not because we are Jerusalem, but because the Creator *G_d* who is Judge presides here. And on these days, peace and reconciliation have come again to all with faith to receive. I can see with my mind, though some say I am way too creative, many peoples and powerful nations coming to this place to entreat *Adonai* for reconciliation, for rain, for life— and mankind living as one. The tower of Babel once again redeemed.

I stand at the appointed place now, facing east. It is blistering hot in the sun. Though my draping clothes protect me from the sun, I am still drenched head to toe by my sweat. There is a breeze, but it is coming off the southeastern desert plains—not very cooling at all. I will not be here very long fortunately. It is my duty, my glory to blow *Yir'eh* one last time. I have wondered what the purpose of the sound of the *shofar* is here at the end of the *Sukkoth*. I think that it is my role to remind the pilgrims why they came—to remind them what they felt *lipne Elohim*. They came to this place as slaves and leave as royalty. They came constipated with guilt, shame, fear, anger, and doubt as divided bickering prodigal sons. They leave purged and unified. They came with significant anxieties of the drought that looms over them. They leave with bellies, and hearts no doubt, filled. I have heard none who lacked anything during this festival. Some say, that there has never been a feast like this one.

I am even feeling more at peace with regard to *Qayin*. There is still much restorative work to be done. But there was a real justice that prevailed—just not the justice that I had imagined. It turned out to be a higher justice, a more substantive justice that *Qayin* could not have paid. *Hevel* experienced an alien *shalom*. *Qayin* as well. No doubt *Tamarah* too—and all the others affected by the crime. In truth, it was the same *shalom*, and glory that we had all experienced two years ago when God's presence came into the Holy of Holies. Today, I feel like a son of G_d. Today, I feel loved, honored, and grateful. Praise be to *G_d!* Praise be to *G_d!* He is good and His love endures forever…He is good and His love endures forever! Amen?

I also think that my *shofar* is given the privilege of being an messenger of good news. The penetrating voice of my darkened-yet-redeemed-from-the-fire *shofar*, *Yir'eh*, no doubt represents the narrative of the glory and presence of *G_d* who is not at all limited to this place but proceeds out and beyond the hills and seas. *G_d* truly does go before His children. His voice is speaking into the

Chaos before they enter. In some sense the sound of the *shofar* has access to the power to break our innate pride and arrogance and to somehow mysteriously empower within us a godly humility and a desire and ability to merely receive the lamb that *G_d* provides for us over and over again.

This day, I also know that both *Hevel* and *Qayin*, wherever they are, will recognize *Yir'eh's* voice and be reminded of the events that occurred over the last three weeks. I know that wherever they hear its voice, they are smiling, something that was impossible only days ago. But now? They may even dance in the wake of justice and her stepsister, reconciliation.

But lastly, and this is what intrigues me most today. I am a representative of the abundant grace of *Adonai*. All who turn their ears may hear his voice without exception. In fact it would be a hard-hearted one who would turn their ear away, choose to not hear His voice. It would be purposely a *high handed* choice, despicable— something that even *Qayin* did not do. The voice of *Yir'eh* calls to all. It calls to the north, south, east and west without exception. The voice fills the ravines, the wells, and the crevices. Its voice rides the distant waves without hindrance.

Rejoice Israel, you are highly favored! The Lord is indeed with us. Speak out *Yir'eh*!

"Hari—ooo" "Hari-oooooo!" "Hari-ooooooooooo!"

After my duties were complete, and I put *Yir'eh* back in its protective linens, I went down to the southern gate of the temple. I had an appointment to dine on freshly baked flat breads with King Silas.

Afterward
(by Dr. Baruch Jr.)

This is where the tale of *Jesiah*, the *shofar* blower must end for now. There are many more stories from *Abba's* repertoire that might be interesting to publish some day, other fun and interesting fictional characters. Do you wonder what became of *Hevel*? What disaster was the prophet speaking about? *Abba* would say, "Tune in next time, same channel, same station." For we Jews, the story is never done.

But I can't help but laugh again remembering *Abba*, the Kosher Indiana Jones, exaggerate the *shofar's* 'hari-ooooooooooo'. His lips protruded into the sky over our beds, over and over again, until all of us joined in and played the imaginary *shofar* along with *Jesiah*. For a moment the entire Baruch clan were *shofar* players—very loud ones. We were the new heralds of *Adonai* to our people. *Abba*, you are deeply missed!

The point of *Abba's* stories is far more than entertainment. Ultimately, he was trying to teach his sons what it looked like, what

175

it felt like to be a *First Temple* Jew.   We are separated from that world by multiple horrific disruptions.   There was the destruction of *Jesiah's First Temple* and Babylonian exile in 586 BCE.   There was the destruction of the Herodian *Second Temple* in 70 CE.   There was most recently the holocaust, and many more tragedies in-between. We are post-post *Second Temple* Jews.   Arguably, there are still great similarities between our two worlds, but there are naturally great defining differences.   Most of the wonderful modern liturgies that we enjoy were penned post-destruction of the *Second Temple* and would be unrecognizable to *Jesiah*.

Great similarities remain of course.   For instance, today we modern Jews, post-*Second Temple* Jews also blow the *shofar* at the onset of *Rosh Hashanah* and the conclusion of *Yom Kippur*.   As it was for the *First Temple* Jews, *Hevel,* and *Jesiah,* the act of blowing explicitly urges us to severely weigh our actions over the last year and to repent, to "abandon evil ways and wicked thoughts."[xxxix]

But there are stark differences.   For *Jesiah*, there was nothing more critical to the Jew than the *shekinah* glory of *G_d* present in the midst of the *Great Temple* in Jerusalem.   All *High Holy Day* rituals, *Rosh Hashanah, Yom Kippur,* and *Sukkoth* revolved around the powerful identity-producing intimate *lipne Elohim*.   G_d <u>was</u> present in Israel.   Imagine.   Personal and corporate redemption of our sins was accomplished virtually all by Him.   All of our many sacrifices ultimately pointed to His single sacrifice that He provided annually on our behalf.   The healing of our whole community was <u>His</u> work; we only watched in amazement, as helpless as our forefathers at the Red Sea.

Our modern liturgies, as poignant and wonderful as they are, must play out in a milieu without a central *Temple*, without an ordained-by-*G_d* High Priest, without an ordained-by-*G_d* King, without ordained-by-*G_d* prophets, and with a people scattered and historically beat-up.

It is obvious why it must be so.   With the *Temple* destroyed, not once but twice, all rituals associated with the *Temple* had to be discontinued.   What else were our ancestors supposed to do?   There had to be atonement for our sins.   The residue of sin had to be purged from our community. So our forefathers did what we would have done. They divined an achievable Torahic solution. There is a famous story told about a conversation between the Great Rabbi Yohanan ben *Zakkai* and one of his disciples Rabbi Joshua shortly after 70 AD as they beheld the *Temple* ruins.

"Woe is us!" cried Rabbi Joshua, "that the place where the iniquities of Israel were atoned for is now laid waste!"

"My son," replied Rabbi *Zakkai*, "Do not be grieved. We have another atonement as effective as this. And what is it? Acts of lovingkindness." [xl]

It is said that by these words Judaism was literally spared death and could live another day, another generation. Without the intentionality and leadership of Rabbi *Zakkai*, Judaism would likely have been absorbed into the nations. Though it survived, and in fact thrived, it had been changed.

Today, the liturgical atmosphere is very different. Modern liturgies, in the absence of a *Temple* and the *shekinah* presence of G_d, provide for us three ways to work to attain atonement: acts of charity, prayer, and repentance. These are good things of course, but are we forever resigned to miss the powerful workings of healing and reconciliation experienced in the *First Temple*? Are we resigned to remain spiritually exiled from the *lipne Elohim*? Are we resigned to not experience such healing, such reconciliation, such forgiveness that *Jesiah* and our ancestors came to expect? Are we resigned to slip into individualism and individual effort to achieve reconciliation with G_d and with each other?

This is our modern reality. Please do not misunderstand. We do not live in the absence of the presence of G_d, for G_d is no doubt always present. But, in our rare moments when we finally shed our deeply rooted corporate blind-spots, we must be aware that we live as a people of G_d without the relational joy, identity and glory that necessarily happens when G_d's *kabod* dwells intrinsically within our midst. *Selah.* But this is one of the reasons that *Abba* told these tales of *Jesiah*. His testimony of such a place and relationship to *G_d* gives us immense hope for a divinely appointed reconciliation in the future.

Being a modern Jew, I also humbly wonder aloud if the harsh violation and victimization of the Babylonian captivity radically changed Israel's understanding of our calling to the *goyim*, to the gentile nations? From the *Temple* confines, Israel was elected by *G_d* to be a light to all of the nations. All of the nations were to come to *G_d* by means of Israel's living witness and testimony as a people of *G_d*. Did we lose some of our missionary fervor?

Jesiah could not imagine that *G_d* would ever abandon His people. *Jesiah* could not ever imagine the possibility of the need for a *Second Temple*. Is it not reasonable that the Babylonian disruption, and then the later Roman Disruption would have had at least some effect on our sense of missional calling? Would it not cause us to even slightly hesitate in the Great *Sukkoth* Dance? I think that *Hevel* would argue that such disruptions and shame would enflame our innate 'slaveness'; it would naturally exacerbate the ever-present internal fear that we must to jump through religious hoop after hoop to earn *G_d*'s elusive favor.

Imagine a child separated from his parents in a crowded mall for hours and hours. The reunion is wonderful, but still the child is changed internally. They no longer have the same child-like wonder, joyfulness and trust as they did before. They are aware of the frightening new possibility of abandonment. Life is now more dangerous than it had been only hours before. Their smile does not come as easy or as often. Can this happen to an entire people? If so, I am of a people that have experienced this abandonment and 'lostness' not once but many times. Imagine the further effect to we modern Jews who are the survivors of the holocaust, which was only a heartbeat ago.

I also wonder if the 'religion' of the returning 6th ct BCE exiles was naturally marred by the reality of that 70 year abandonment. Their naïveté was gone, stripped away. I do not judge our forefathers or their intentions. In fact, I would proclaim them heroic and faithful for returning to the land and rebuilding Jerusalem. But I wonder if a sense of isolationism naturally seeped into the mindset of our ancestors that has subtly robbed us of much of the proactive G_d-calling that was ours. I wonder if a strain of legalism and moralism naturally penetrated the liturgy and teachings of the *Second Temple* of Ezra and Nehemiah? Was our well-meaning 'fencing of the Torah' to some degree a protective mechanism driven by the backwash of the exile? Was it to some degree the best that an orphaned people could imagine? After all, there is no evidence in the prophets or the oral tradition that the *shekinah* glory of G_d came back with us. What would *Jesiah* have thought about his role without the *shekinah* of G_d present in the *Holy of Holies*?

As a Jew, hearing the story of *Jesiah's* day, and the visceral present and active role of G_d in the midst of His people, I mourn the loss of something that was our inheritance during these *High Holy Days*. *Jesiah* represents a lost era to us. It was a time when we did not seek atonement on our own as individuals, but together, as a community *lipne Elohim*. It seems to me that *Jesiah* was aware of the importance of the presence of G_d to empower change in Israel, to empower our individual and corporate repentance, our reconciliation and healing. How are we to accomplish these things, our calling, without G_d's *kabod*? Spiritually speaking, I wonder that though we are in the land again at last, perhaps we are still in spiritual exile? I humbly offer this as a beginning of a dialogue, not a criticism or conclusion. What were we to do?

But *Jesiah's* G_d, my G_d, the G_d of Israel has not given up. He might turn His back for a time. Ezekiel not only *'yir-eh'd'* G_d's *kabod* leaving the *Temple*, but he foresaw its return in glory. Listen my people.

Then the man brought me to the gate facing east, and I saw the glory of the G_d of Israel coming from the east. His voice was like the roar of rushing waters, and the land was radiant with his glory. The vision I saw was like the vision I had seen when he came to destroy the city and like the visions I had seen by the Kebar River, and I fell facedown. The glory of the LORD entered the Temple through the gate facing east. Then the Spirit lifted me up and brought me into the inner court, and the glory of the LORD filled the Temple. While the man was standing beside me, I heard

179

someone speaking to me from inside the Temple. He said: "Son of man, this is the place of my throne and the place for the soles of my feet. This is where I will live among the Israelites forever. The house of Israel will never again defile my holy name — neither they nor their kings — by their prostitution and the lifeless idols of their kings at their high places. When they placed their threshold next to my threshold and their doorposts beside my doorposts, with only a wall between me and them, they defiled my holy name by their detestable practices. So I destroyed them in my anger. Now let them put away from me their prostitution and the lifeless idols of their kings, and I will live among them forever. (Ezekiel 43:1-9 NIV)

It is worth pointing out that all of *Abba's* surviving sons have pursued active relationships with *G_d* as good Jews. Three of us have become keen followers of the Jew Jesus. Personally, I know of no other man who emanates *First Temple Torah* more than Him. I follow Him because I believe that it makes me a better Jew, though some of my brothers would graciously disagree. Believe me, *Abba's* legacy of late night 'discussions' with our Rabbi continues. *Selah!*

It is also only fitting that I, his eldest son would follow in his sandals as an archaeologist, though of far less renown. In fact, as this book heads to the publisher, we are only a matter of weeks, maybe days from entering the recently discovered mausoleum tomb of *Herod the Great. Abba* would be so proud.

Selah!

Dr. Ehud Baruch Jr.
22nd of *Tishri*, 5769

Glossary of Terms

Abba- Intimate term for father, poppa, daddy.

Abiathar- Descendent from Eli, the only of the priests who escaped the slaughter of the priests of Nob by Saul. He fled to David at Keilah. He served under David and Solomon until banished for supporting Adonijah (1 Sam 15:24, 29, 35, 20:35, 1 Kings 1:7, 19, 25, 2:22, 26).

Adonai- Lord. Orthodox Jews will not utter the Holy Name of G_d. Instead when they read G_d, they will verbalize "Adonai".

Al-Aqsa Mosque- Literally: 'the Farthest Mosque.' It is also popularly called by Muslims the '*al-Haram ash-Sharif*' or '*Sacred Noble Sanctuary*.' Mosques are places of worship in Islam. But this mosque is considered to be the third holiest site in all Islam. It is located on the very site of King Solomon's Temple complex in Jerusalem. Muslims believe that Mohammed was transported from the Sacred Mosque in Mecca to al-Aqsa during his legendary night journey.

ʿaliyah- Literally 'going up'. The pilgrimage of Jews for the three great annual festivals was called an *ʿaliyah*. They are going up to be with G_d in the Temple.

ʿamal- harsh labor, toil. Not used for generic tasks, or careers. It carries a negative connotation.

ʿani- 'Affliction'- Hebrew *ʿani* (pronounced 'a-nee'). The root of the word *ʿani* carries the idea of someone greater forcing their will upon someone weaker. These are unwilling victims. This includes the forcing of one into submission—to make someone low, or to subjugate them against their will. In verb form it is often glossed 'afflict', 'humiliate', 'humble', 'to punish' or 'inflict pain upon'. In noun form *ʿoni*, it could be glossed as 'affliction' or 'poverty. *ʿAni* in noun form would be the afflicted themselves, or the poor.

Antiphonally- responsively. In ritual settings, it was common to have choirs of priests facing each other singing as if having a choral conversation between them.

181

THE JESIAH SCROLLS

Ark of the Covenant- Gold-covered Holy Vessel within the Holy of Holies that contained the two tablets of the law, some manna and Aaron's blossoming rod. The *shekinah* of G_d dwelt above its cover, the mercy seat, in-between the statue of two Cherubim.

Araunah- Jebusite owner of the threshing floor purchased by David to be the location of the Temple of *G_d*. See 2 Samuel 24:16.

'asham- The *'asham* is the 'guilt offering'. It is a subcategory of *'olahs*, where the supplicant brings an animal to the altar, personally prepares the sacrifice, and is implicitly saying publicly, to the victim and all Israel, "For my crime, this is what I really deserve!" No denial here. Then the animal is totally burned up as an *'olah*. There is nothing left. The guilt is up in smoke. It is finished. The perpetrator is privately and publicly saying, "I take full responsibility for my choices and actions. I am committed to making it right—i.e., justified."

Asaph- Asaph was a prominent Levite Priest and one of the leaders of David's choir. See 1Chr. 6:39; 25:1; 2Chr. 20:14 and Ezra 2:41.

Azazel-
> *"Aaron is to offer the bull for his own sin offering to make atonement for himself and his household. Then he is to take the two goats and present them before the LORD at the entrance to the Tent of Meeting. He is to cast lots for the two goats— one lot for the LORD and the other for the scapegoat (Azazel). Aaron shall bring the goat whose lot falls to the LORD and sacrifice it for a sin offering. But the goat chosen by lot as the scapegoat shall be presented alive before the LORD to be used for making atonement by sending it into the desert as a scapegoat (Azazel). Aaron shall bring the bull for his own sin offering to make atonement for himself and his household, and he is to slaughter the bull for his own sin offering."*
> *(Lev 16:6-11)*

On the day of Atonement, the High Priest, after first performing the prescribed sacrifices for himself and his family, offers three animals as atonement for the people. There was the ram for a burnt offering, and two goats for a sin-offering. Having brought the goats before the people, he cast lots for them, the one lot 'for Yahweh,' and the other 'for Azazel.' The goat that fell to Yahweh was offered as a sin-offering for the people. But the goat of Azazel (now usually known as the 'scapegoat') was made the subject of a more striking ceremony. The high priest laid his hands upon its head and confessed over it the sins of the people. Then the goat for Azazel, which effectively took upon itself all of the sins and sin residue of the people and the Temple was then led into the desert never to be seen again. The cryptic name 'Azazel' has continued to confound scholars. Some Rabbis suggest the etymology of the word being 'Azaz' (rugged), and 'el' (strong), and refer it to the rugged and rough mountain cliff from which the goat was cast down (Yoma 67b; Sifra, Aḥare, ii. 2; Targ. Yer. Lev. xiv. 10, and most medieval commentators). Others suggest that Azazel was a 'se'erim', a goat like desert demon or jinn that ruled the wilderness extreme. The sins of the people were cast into the region of the demonic where it belonged.

Azariah- In Hebrew means 'G_d helps'.

Ba'al- Ba'al was the god of rain, thunder and lightning and often fertility and agriculture worshipped by many of the Semitic tribes in the region of Israel. In the Bible, the term *'Ba'al'* often was used to refer to any of many false local spirit-deities worshipped in competition with Adonai. The word *ba'al* can also refers to any human master or lord. The slavemasters in Egypt were *ba'als* to the Israel slaves. The term almost always carries a negative connotation of a capricious overlord.

Babylon- Perennial superpower in the Middle East. One of the great powers of the 'east'. Conquered Judah and destroyed the *First Temple* in 586 BCE.

Bara'- *Bara'* is to 'create', but in the Hebrew Qal tense it is only used of G_d creating out of nothing. "In the beginning, G_d *'bara'd'* (created) the heaven and the earth." It is a 'creative proclamation.'

Bathsheba- Wife of Uriah the Hittite whom David raped. She became the mother of Solomon.

Bin, Binah- The Hebrew word *'bin'* (pronounced 'bean') and its derivatives such as *binah* (pronounced 'bean-ah') are related to the concept of understanding or discernment. It would broadly include our current notion of 'good old common sense'. But more specifically, *bin* and *binah* are gifts of G_d to choose between two paths by weighing the consequences of both decisions.

Booths- On the 15ᵗʰ of Tishri, all Israel is called to live in *Sukkoth* (temporary shelters or booths) for seven days as part of the Great Feast of Booths (also called Tabernacles, or 'The Party') as a commemoration of G_d saving Israel from Egypt. "Live in booths for seven days: All native-born Israelites are to live in booths so your descendants will know that I had the Israelites live in booths when I brought them out of Egypt. I am the LORD your G_d.'" (Lev 23:42-3).

Cereal Offering- The cereal offering is prescribed in Lev 2. It is made up of grain, most likely barley, crushed into fine flour bound together with virgin olive oil and baked into cakes. The cereal offering is also known as the poor man's offering. If one could not afford an animal, one could bring a cereal offering. Only a token of the offering was actually burned on the altar. The priests would eat the rest as part of their allotment.

Central Valley- Also called the 'Tyropean Valley.' It is the north-south swale or depression that ran on the western side of the ancient City of David and provided for much of the sewage draining for city into the Valley of Hinnom. Due to construction and land fill over the centuries the Central Valley is hardly noticeable to untrained eyes today.

Chaos- In Genesis 1:1-3 where we read, "In the beginning G_d created the heavens and the earth. Now the earth was formless and empty, darkness was over the surface of the deep, and the Spirit of G_d was hovering over the waters. And G_d said, 'Let there be light,' and there was light [NIV]." 'Formless and empty' (Hebrew- tohu vevohu) is the Hebrew concept for chaos. It is imaged as a raging ocean or flood. It is into it that G_d unhindered speaks the ordered foundation from which life can thrive. In the creation legends of other ancient Semitic cultures, Chaos is an actually entity that continually threatens the heavens with destruction of the current order. In recent finds from ancient Ugarit, there is a poem in which Ba'al fights the sons of Atirat and defeats them by 'smiting them on the shoulders' and then rises to the throne of his Kingdom (III AB V 1-6 of the Ras Shamra texts. See Hans-Joachim Kraus, *Psalms 60-150: A Continental Commentary* (Minneapolis: Fortress Press, 1993) p. 235.

Chasidim- Chasidic Jews are one of the branches of modern Orthodox Judaism. There is no single shape or form or Chasidism. Chasidic communities tend to combine ritual piety, scholarly study of the writings, devotion to the community Rabbi, personal and communal purity with the mystical teachings of the 18th Century Israel ben Eliezer.

Cherubim- Angelic beings who dwell in the presence of G_d in the heavenlies. Their likeness was placed on top of the Ark of the Covenant in the Holy of Holies.

Chislev- Ninth month of the Hebrew calendar, roughly corresponding to November/December in our western calendars.

Coronation of God Event- Many scholars, both Jewish and Christian have suggested that the first of Tishri in the First Temple period was celebrated as a divine coronation day; some pointing to Psalms 93-100 being the specific liturgy for such an event. "In these particular psalms, the shofar sound is a joyous proclamation of God's ascendency to the kingship and has none of the other connotations it received in later Jewish thought."[xli] The practice is not specifically noted in the Bible, but the implicit case is strong and so has been added to this narrative.

Cubit- 1 cubit is roughly equivalent to 1.65 ft.

Day of Atonement: Also referred to as the *Day of Purgation* and *Yom Kippur*. It is held annually on the 10th of the month of *Tishri*. According to our Jewish calendars, days begin at sunset and go to sunset on the following day. So the *Day of Atonement* actually begins in the evening. This is the most sacred and ritually important day for the Jews all over the world in our time. It is very clear that it was also extremely important for Israel during the Iron Age II Kings.

Day of Purgation- See *Day of Atonement* and *Yom Kippur*.

Dome of the Rock- Golden-domed Islamic Shrine on the Temple Mount.

Elohim- Plural form of 'El', one of the more common ancient titles for any deity and in the Bible, the most common form of the name of the Hebrew *G_d*. Can also refer to gods (plural).

En-Gedi- Famous oasis in the Bible. Near the Dead Sea. Known for its springs and beautiful flora and fauna.

Fifth Scroll- The Books of Deuteronomy.

First Commonwealth- The period of the Kings of Israel spanning the time from the kingships of Saul and David in the eleventh century BCE to the destruction of Jerusalem by the Babylonians in 586 BCE.

First Temple- Solomon's Temple, built around 980 BCE on the Mount of Moriah overlooking the ancient City of David on the plot of land that

185

David purchased from Araunah the Jebusite. As recorded in 2 Chronicles 7, the *shekinah* glory of *G_d* entered the *First Temple* in a powerful and visceral way. The *First Temple* was destroyed in 586 BCE by the Babylonians. The prophet Ezekiel records the testimony of *G_d's shekinah* glory abandoning the *First Temple* (Ezekiel 10).

Fourth Scroll- The book of Numbers.

Fountain Gate- Gate from the lower Kidron Valley into the southeastern section of the City of David, near the pool of Siloam.

Frankincense- Frankincense is a fragrant gum resin widely considered the Boswellia tree sap native to the Eastern coast of Africa. It was a very expensive spice.

Gamala- 'Camel hump'. Ancient fortified city in ancient Syria, modern Golan Heights. It is built on a mountain ridge that is wedged in a strategic valley. From the mountains around it looks like a camel's hump.

Gihon- Spring that is the water source for the ancient city of Jerusalem.

G_d- *Jesiah*, being a righteous priest, would never say or pen the unspeakable Name of *G_d* (referred to today as the 'tetragrammaton'). We understand that the Name is only uttered by the High Priest and only then on the *Day of Atonement* as specifically prescribed by *Torah* and tradition. Instead, he regularly appropriately uses the simple two Hebrew consonants ("), which were vocalized *'Adonai'*— or in English 'Lord'.

Great Altar- The *'mizbe'ach'*, the large altar in the Temple courtyard. The top was used to burn the various sacrifices. The walls of the altar were used for the sprinkling the blood of certain sacrifices. It was accessed by a series of ramps, built on its southern side. The Altar was made of small perfectly smooth stones, lime, pitch, and glazing.

Hatti- By the time of Solomon, the formerly ancient and great Hittite Empire was in some disarray, and yet still a feared powerhouse in the region. At its peak, it encompassed much of Anatolia (modern Turkey), Lebanon, and Syria.

Hevel- The second born of Adam and Eve (Genesis 4), the first recorded murder victim, murdered due to the jealousy of his elder brother Cain

(Qayin). His name means 'having little substance or worth', also 'vapor' or 'meaninglessness'.

Ha-Melekh ha-Kadosh- The Holy King

Herod the Great- King of the Roman province of Israel from 37 to 4 BCE. He is responsible for the rebuilding and expanding the *Second Temple* of Ezra and Nehemiah into the Great Temple so familiar to many of us today.

High Holy Days- The very important 10 *Days of Awe* from the First to Tenth of Tishri. Includes *Rosh Hashanah* and *Yom Kippur*. It is on these days that all Israel is called to humbly consider their lives and relationship with *G_d* and man for the previous year.

Hinnom Valley- The deep valley south of the hills comprising Jerusalem; it joins with the Central Valley and the Kidron Valley at a point immediately south of the City of David and runs southeast ultimately purging into the Dead Sea. By the time of the New Testament, the valley had become a bit of a trash heap filled with unmanageable refuse from the urbanized Jerusalem and often used fires to burn the worst of the garbage. In the 1st century CE it has become an analogy to eternal punishment, Gehennah, the place of purging fires.

High Handed Sins- In Numbers 15, there is a legal distinction made between 'unintentional' and 'intentional' sins. The latter category is referred to as 'high handed' sin in the Hebrew. In Numbers 15:30 we read, "But anyone who sins defiantly, whether native-born or alien, blasphemes the LORD, and that person must be cut off from his people." Scholars widely debate what the categories technically refer to. It appears that the rubric 'unintentional' may include 1) sins that a person does though they are unaware (or ignorant) that it is a Biblical crime, 2) sins – such as touching dead things unaware—which the person isn't even aware that they have done until after the event (and then they feel remorse), or even 3) sins that have occurred by choice which later the perpetrator becomes remorseful for. In the latter case, the perpetrator acts out of gross insensitivity to the Law or others, or perhaps blindspots—but when they are made aware of the Law and the crime, they are repentant. A good example of this is David's crime with Bathsheba in 2 Samuel 12. When Nathan's parable is used to make David emotionally and morally aware of his choices, David repents. Technically then, this would also fit in the legal rubric of 'unintentional' sin. But there is another category of

187

defiant, *high handed* crimes (Numbers 15:30), which appears to be the crimes of a person who knowingly sins against G_d, mankind and creation and is not at all repentant.

Scholars debate how this notion of 'high handed' sins fits with the notion of the offerings of the Day of Atonement covering all sins. Broad descriptor for 'all' sins seen in the Temple instructions only in Leviticus 16:16 and 16:21 (with the preposition 'concerning'), Lev 16:30 and 34 (with the preposition 'from' or 'with') and perhaps referred to in two period Psalms, Psalm 25:18 (of David) and 85:2 (Sons of Korah). This is a very encouraging 'all'. It is noteworthy that the phrase is also in Deuteronomy 9:18, as Moses testifies of his successful efforts to assuage G_d's wrath for all the sins of the people—an early atonement by a savior/prophet. Micah 7:19 is interesting for our purposes. He was one of the last prophets before the fall of Samaria and so rightly fits within the pre-exilic mindset. He says this, "Who is a G_d like you, who pardons sin and forgives the transgression of the remnant of his inheritance? You do not stay angry forever but delight to show mercy. You will again have compassion on us; you will tread our sins underfoot and hurl all our iniquities into the depths of the sea." (Micah 7:18-19)

Hinneh- "Behold!" "Look!"

Holy Place- The Holy Place of the Tabernacle included the golden altar of incense, the table of showbread and the golden lampstand. At the heart of the Holy Place and separated by a thick curtain was the cubical Holy of Holies and the place where G_d's glory dwelt over the Ark of the Covenant. Only the priests were allowed in and only after they had ritually washed their hands and feet outside. The Holy Place was about 30 feet long, 15 feet wide and 15 feet high.

Holy of Holies- The *Holy of Holies* is a small 15 by 15 foot room separated from the Holy Place by a woven thick veil. It housed the Ark of the Covenant. G_d's *shekinah* glory dwelt between the Cherubim on the top of the Mercy Seat. Only the High Priest once a year on the Day of Atonement could enter the Holy of Holies.

Ichabod- Literally '*Ichabod*' translates 'No glory'. During one of the worst defeats ever recorded by Israel (see 1 Samuel 4), not only did Israel lose 30,000 foot soldiers, and the High Priest Eli, and his two sons perished— but also more catastrophic than these, the Philistines captured the Ark of the Covenant. At this very moment, the daughter-in-law of Eli gave birth to a son and named him 'G_d's *kabod* is departed' –literally '*Ichabod*'.

Innui Nefesh- This 'self-denial' (*'innui nefesh'* in the Hebrew) is literally 'afflicting one's soul'. This is commanded in the *Torah* specifically on *Yom Kippur*. In Leviticus 23:26-8, we read, "The Lord said to Moses, 'The tenth day of this seventh month is the *Day of Atonement*. Hold a sacred assembly and deny yourselves (lit. 'afflict your soul') and present an offering made to the Lord by fire. Do no work on that day, because it is the *Day of Atonement*, when atonement is made for you before the LORD your *G_d*.'" This 'deny yourself' can include numerous things depending upon its context. Minimally it refers to fasting, but may also include wearing coarse clothing, going without comfortable shoes and abstaining from other enjoyments such as sex.

Iron Age II- Archaeological term to describe the period in the Middle East from the tenth to sixth centuries BCE. See First Commonwealth Period. This was the age when those who had iron smelting capacities achieved technical superiority in the region.

Isis- One of the many Egyptian gods that the Israelites would have been exposed to. She is the goddess of motherhood and fertility, the mother of Horus.

Jebus- The ancient Jebusite name of the city of Jerusalem before David conquered it and renamed it 'Jerusalem' or 'The City of David.'

Kabod- *Kabod* (pronounced ka-vod) is the Hebrew word for 'glory'. Maybe the most familiar passage that refers to *G_d's kabod* is in Exodus 33:18ff, where *G_d's kabod* passes before Moses. It is likely derived from the word for weight, but came to mean social worth. We have the idiom that a person of power and authority, 'throws their weight around'. *G_d* is the highest of 'weightiness', meaning that no person has more glory than Him. *G_d* innately is *kabod* and gives it to others as He chooses. In 1 Kings 8:10-11, we read about *G_d's kabod*, actually physically entering the *Holy Place* in Solomon's Temple during the national festival of *Sukkoth* (Booths) on the 15th of *Tishri*. See also 2 Chronicles 5:13-14 and 7:1-3. This is similar to the account of *G_d's* glory entering the wilderness tabernacle. See Exodus 40:34.

Kebar River- River in ancient Babylon. The place where Ezekiel was given his vision from *G_d*.

Kidron Valley- The valley that runs roughly north-south along the eastern side of Jerusalem. It divides Jerusalem from the Mount of Olives to the east. It joins with the Hinnom valley at the southern base of the ancient City of David.

Kohen, kohanim- The Hebrew for priest is *'kohen'* pronounced 'co-hayn' and plural priests, *'kohanim'*, pronounced 'co-ha-neem'

Korah- The sons of *Korah* were Levites, priests who had been chosen by David for the ministry of music at the Temple. "These are the men David put in charge of the music in the house of the LORD after the ark came to rest there. They ministered with music before the tabernacle, the Tent of Meeting, until Solomon built the Temple of the LORD in Jerusalem. They performed their duties according to the regulations laid down for them." (1 Chr 6:31-2)

Kotel- The Israeli descriptor for the Western Wall.

Levites- Descendents of Levi, the second born of Jacob. They received no physical inheritance (i.e., land) when Israel returned to the Promised Land under Joshua. Their inheritance was to lead Israel in the worship of *G_d*. Their livelihood came from offerings. Though not all descendents of Levi are priests (*kohanim*), all legitimate *kohanim* must come from the tribe of Levi. The Levite's principal roles in the liturgy included singing Psalms and playing instruments during Temple services, performing construction and maintenance for the Temple, serving as guards, and performing other services. There were Levites who lived and worked in areas beyond Jerusalem. They generally served as teachers and judges and overseers of the cities of refuge.

Lipne Elohim- Literally, *'lipne Elohim'* (pronounced *lip- nay- El-o-heem*), can mean many things. It can be 'in the very experiential presence of *G_d*', 'before the face of *G_d*', 'in front of *G_d*' and the like. But in the context of the *High Holy Days*, it often has the technical reference to coming into an official audience with *G_d* as the Great Judge or King. In this sense it is not merely locative (referring to a specific location) but purposive (referring to the reason for coming to *G_d*). In today's parlance, imagine coming to court for a court date. You are said to come before the Judge on that day. It is a metonymy (a poetic device which uses a single part to refer to the whole) for all of the events of the trial.

Ma'at- The Egyptian god of truth, justice order and balance.

190

Melee Infantry- Close combat foot soldiers.

Mishloach- Perhaps this is best translated 'the sending away (free).' For a similar event in rural Arabic settings, see Irani, G., & Funk, N. (2000, August), "Rituals of reconciliation: Arab-Islamic Perspectives," Kroc Institute Occasional Paper #19:OP:2.

Mishnah- From the Hebrew 'instruction'. Collection of oral tradition, teaching, and exegesis which was officially collected at the Council of Jamnia (90 CE), and edited and redacted by Rabbis Akiba and Judah ha-Nasi by the early 3rd Century CE. The 'instructions' come from well-preserved oral sources. The *Mishnah* provides important insight into the religion of Judaism and the liturgy of the Temple particularly in the *Second Temple* period. From our western perspective, the *Mishnah* appears to be a compilation of brief, terse legal opinions and debates between scholars.

Mitzvah- A good deed performed out of religious duty.

Mizrak- The '*mizrak*' was one of the Holy vessels for use in sacrifices. Blood was considered life and was not to be discarded. All life was valuable to G_d. The *mizrak* was a deep containment vessel—or bowl with a handle attached—made of gold and equipped with a long handle that protruded from the top. It could be held under the cut in the bull's or lamb's throat to catch the blood that ran out. No doubt multiple *mizraks* were required for an animal the size of a young bull.

Negev- Semi-desert region of southern Israel. Includes the patriarchal home of Abraham, Beersheba.

'Olah- The '*olah* (Hebrew for 'going up'—pronounced 'o- lah') is a broad category for regular burnt offerings. '*Olahs* are totally burned on the altar, totally given to G_d to pay judicially for the supplicant's crimes of omission and commission against G_d, mankind or creation. The name probably comes from the image of the smoke that is 'going up' to G_d. Leviticus 1 gives instructions for the '*olah*.

Ophel- The southern side of the Temple Mount was referred in the Bible as the 'Ophel' (the high place) - meaning the upper city (acropolis) of ancient Jerusalem.

Palanquin- A covered litter for a reclining passenger, carried on four poles on the shoulders of four or more bearers.

Pharaoh- The King of Egypt. Considered divine by the Egyptians.

Qayin- *Qayin*, Cain was the first born of Adam (See Genesis 4), the murdering unrepentant brother of Abel (Hevel). *Qayin* remained unrepentant even when *G_d* gave him multiple opportunities to admit what he did and be healed. This was the first '*high handed*' sin. Every young Jew knows of the story of *Qayin* and *Hevel* from Gen 4. *Qayin* comes from *qana'*— which means 'to bring forth' or 'to possess'—maybe the implication of control and self-sufficiency? *Hevel* in popular use refers to 'vapor' or perhaps 'worthlessness'. In a jealous self-centered rage, *Qayin*, though warned by *G_d* murders his twin brother in cold blood. Though his trial is recorded in Genesis 4, there is no resolution of justice. His first defense was the unfortunate question to *G_d*, "Am I my brother's keeper?" *Qayin* was allowed to run into the wilderness to live far away from *Adonai* and justice.

Qorban- The '*qorban*' (pronounced 'kor-ban') is a 'drawing near' sacrifice—or also referred to as an 'audience sacrifice'. In the ancient world, it serves as a formal request by a human supplicant for an audience with *G_d* (i.e., *lipne Elohim*). This is not to say that the Creator Lord of Israel requires such a bribe or encouragement from our hands. It is a recognized Middle Eastern cultural protocol, where the lesser person acknowledges the greatness of the other. The supplicant, the one who approaches *G_d* is reminded that they are in audience only at the pleasure of *G_d*.

Ra- The hawk-headed Egyptian Sun god.

Rabbi's Tunnel- Work on the so-called 'Rabbi's Tunnel', named such because it was the work of Orthodox rabbis began shortly after the Six Day War in 1967, nominally under the Ministry of Religious Affairs. It led to violent riots when at last discovered in 1982. The untrained rabbis had dug a narrow horizontal mine from the Western Wall plaza north along the outside of the western wall of the Temple Mount compound. Apparently the rabbis worked with some governmental knowledge but virtually no official oversight. Professional archaeologists steered clear of the clandestine project. In 1982, the rabbis made a startling discovery, a previously unknown ancient sealed underground gate. As they broke through the gate and began to clear out chambers beneath the Temple

Mount, they were heard by Palestinian workmen on top of the Temple Mount through an open cistern. A riot resulted with many people injured and international press involved. A fragile agreement was negotiated between officials that allowed the rabbis to continue their excavations along the outside of the retaining wall. The now-called 'Hasmonean Tunnel' opened to tourists in 1988, runs along the entire length of the western wall.

Rosh Hashanah- The First of Tishri, generally considered today to be the Jewish New Year Celebration and the beginning of the 10 *Days of Awe*. In the *First Temple* period, it was probably more complex of a celebration which celebrated the enthronement of *G_d* upon His eternal throne. According to Moshe Segal, the pre-exilic High Holy Day observed "[t]hree principles, the creation of the world on the New Year, the manifestation of *G_d's* kingship over the world on the New Year, and the judgment of the world by *G_d* on the New Year... *G_d* as Creator, *G_d* as King, *G_d* as judge" (In Moshe Segal, "The Religion of Israel Before Sinai", *Jewish Quarterly Review* 52 (1963):242 in Reuven Hammer, *Entering the High Holy Days: A Complete Guide to the History, Prayers, and Themes,* (Philadelphia: The Jewish Publication Society, 1998), p. 4). Later *Second Temple* practice did not emphasize the psalms in the New Years Liturgy (see Leon F. Liebreich, "Aspects of the New Years Liturgy", *Hebrew Union College Annual* 34 (1963): 175-176). It is suggested that Psalms 93-100 were originally part of the *First Temple G_d*-enthronement liturgy.

Sacred Scrolls- Reference to the Five Scrolls of the Torah (Genesis, Exodus, Leviticus, Numbers and Deuteronomy).

Samachti – Psalm 122. Literally the 'rejoicing'.

Sanhedrin- Generically speaking the term covered the entire Jewish judicial/court system made up of local bodies of elders who would 'sit at the gate of the city' all the way up to the highest appeal, the Great Sanhedrin, the supreme religious body in Israel during the *Second Temple* period. It is unclear exactly when the Great Sanhedrin was formed. The earliest documented record of the Sanhedrin officially meeting was in 57 BCE. According to Rabbinic sources the Great Sanhedrin was made up of 71 sages who met in the Chamber of Hewn Stones in the Temple. The Great Sanhedrin met during the daytime, and did not meet on the Sabbath, festival days or eves. It was led by the 'nasi', president and the vice-president called the 'av bet din'. During its hey day, it was the final authority on Jewish law. Those who went against its ruling could be put

to death as heretics. Its power varied widely due to its relationship with ruling government during the period.
Second Scroll- The Book of Exodus

Second Scroll- The Book of Exodus

Second Temple- The *First Temple* was destroyed in 586 BCE by the Babylonians and the people of Judah scattered into exile. Decrees by the Persian Kings Cyrus the Great (538 BCE) and Darius (521 BCE) made the reconstruction of the Temple possible. In 516 BCE under the leadership of Ezra and Nehemiah, the *Second Temple* was rebuilt on the former site of the Temple of Solomon. It is worth noting that there is no witness that the *shekinah* glory of G_d ever came upon the *Second Temple* as it did both the Wilderness Tabernacle (Exodus 40:35) and the *First Temple* of Solomon (2 Chronicles 7:1-3). The prophet Ezekiel makes note of the *shekinah* glory of G_d leaving the *First Temple* in his tragic vision recorded in Chapter 10. The *Second Temple* was greatly refurbished and expanded during the reign of King Herod beginning around 20 BCE. The *Second Temple* was finally destroyed by the Romans in 70 CE.

Segullah- *Segullah* (pronounced 'seg-oo-lah') is the emperor's special treasure that He personally spends for things that he desires. The NIV glosses it 'special treasure' in Ex 19:5. G_d says to Israel at *Sinai*, "And now, if you will diligently listen to me and keep my covenant, then you will be my special possession (*segullah*) out of all the nations, for all the earth is mine, and you will be to me a kingdom of *kohen*s and a holy nation." (NIV) Someone has called it the Emperor's pocket change—not a belittling comment, but one that speaks of it being his special treasure that is for intimate personal use.

Selah- Unknown meaning. Could be an accepted poetic marker that identifies breaks in movements. Could be the equivalent of a period to end a thought or a paragraph. Some have suggested that it means to 'look up'.

Senir- One of the tall mountains in the Anti-Lebanon range north of Israel. Often used synonymously with Mt. Hermon.

Sheba- Unidentified Iron Age Kingdom. Some scholars suggest that it was Ethiopia, others say Saudi Arabia or perhaps modern Yemen.

Shabbat- Jewish celebration of the seventh day (Friday night to Saturday) of rest as prescribed in the Torah. In modern practice, this is an intimate family time of lighting candles and family devotion.

Shebat- Eleventh month of the Hebrew calendar, roughly corresponding to January/February in our western calendars. Generally the months with the most significant rainfall in the region. See note under *Tishri* regarding rain in the region.

Shekinah- According to Rabbis, it means 'he caused to dwell', signifying a divine visitation of the specific presence of G_d among mankind. The *shekinah* was first witnessed during the Exodus as a cloudy pillar in the day and a fiery pillar by night: "After leaving Succoth they camped at Etham on the edge of the desert. By day the LORD went ahead of them in a pillar of cloud to guide them on their way and by night in a pillar of fire to give them light, so that they could travel by day or night. Neither the pillar of cloud by day nor the pillar of fire by night left its place in front of the people" (Exodus 13:20-22).The *shekinah* left a visible expression upon the face of Moses after and extended audience with G_d (Exodus 34:29). It was visible to all Israel at Mt Sinai (Exodus 24:16), the filling of the Tabernacle (Num 16:42) and *First Temple* (2 Chronicles 7:1). See also 'Kabod'.

Sheol- The grave, death.

Shofar- Ritual music instrument typically made out of a ram's horn.

Siloam- A public pool at the southern tip of the City of David.

Sinai- The Mountain to which G_d brought His people after the Exodus.

Sukkoth- The Great fall festival, held for an entire week beginning on the 15th of Tishri. It coincided with the finalization of the final harvest of the year. It was a time of prescribed gathering in Jerusalem for all Israel. "Celebrate the Feast of Tabernacles for seven days after you have gathered the produce of your threshing floor and your winepress. Be joyful at your Feast — you, your sons and daughters, your menservants and maidservants, and the Levites, the aliens, the fatherless and the widows who live in your towns. For seven days celebrate the Feast to the LORD your G_d at the place the LORD will choose. For the LORD your G_d will bless you in all your harvest and in all the work of your hands, and your joy will be complete (Dt 16:13-15)." Also see 'Booths'.

195

THE JESIAH SCROLLS

Suzerain- A king of kings, an emperor of multiple nations or city states.

Talmud – The important collection of rabbinic discussions pertaining to Jewish law, ethics, philosophy, customs and history. Made up of the *Mishnah* (early 3rd ct. CE) and the Gemara (6th ct, CE). Before the *Second Temple*'s destruction in 70 CE, scholarship in Judaism was driven by the written law (Torah) and the oral traditions of the Rabbinic scholars and teachers faithfully passed down by their disciples. Once the Temple was destroyed, the oral traditions needed to be gathered, authenticated, and written for subsequent generations. The *Mishnah* was the first to be published followed by the Gemara, which contains further discussion and debate regarding issues raised by the *Mishnah*.

Tamarah- Fictional character. Name means 'palm tree'.

Tammuz- Fourth month in the Hebrew calendar. Roughly June and July in our western calendars.

Tanach- The Hebrew Bible.

Tebeth- Tenth month of the Hebrew calendar, roughly corresponding to December/January in our western calendars. Tebeth is normally the beginning of the rainy season.

Temple Mount- Mount Moriah. The mountain plateau just north of the original City of David. It was on this sight that Solomon built the Great *First Temple* complex, which Herod expanded for the *Second Temple* and the place that now contains the *Al-Aqsa Mosque* complex. It is also believed to be the geographic location of Abraham's sacrifice of Isaac (Genesis 17), of the visitation of the angel to King David at the threshing floor of Araunah the Jebusite in (2 Samuel 24) and some believe that it is from here that G_d took the dirt to form Adam and Eve (Genesis 1-2).

Tishri- The seventh month of the Hebrew calendar. Roughly coincides with September/October in our calendars. Rain showers are not unheard of during the month of Tishri but are rather rare—and typically localized showers. Rain is largely predictable in Israel. They live and die by the winter rains, which begin in late December and may extend to March. Generally speaking, the rest of the calendar is semi-arid desert weather (with some regional exceptions). Many scholars suggest that one of the purposes that these *High Holy Days* serve are to pray to G_d for winter rain which means life to Israel. Israel's economy was primarily agricultural based: olives, figs, dates, barley, and wheat. They each depend on regular winter rains.

Tohu ve-Vohu- See *Chaos.*

Torah- The first five books of the Bible.

Tsedaqah- Glossed 'righteousness'. It has a broad range of meanings, but at its core biblically, it refers to a sacrificial 'other-mindedness'. The Righteous man or woman holds community well-being over their own. They are innately hospitable, sacrificial, and charitable. If they have two tunics, they are willing to give one to another who is in need. In legal contexts, it can be synonymous with 'mercy' or the willingness to provide a legal substitute for the crime's penalty.

Valley Gate- Gate into the southwest section of Jerusalem.

Wadi- Regional term for streams. But the word carries the connotation of inherent danger. In the semi-arid region of Israel, there are many dry riverbeds that flash flood when rains come. Wadis can be violent and dangerous during flash floods.

Western Wall- Also called the 'Wailing Wall'. The only remaining part of the retaining wall of Herod's Great Temple complex. Jews consider the sight very holy. It is the closest they can come to the place where the *shekinah* glory of G_d once dwelt. Jews will come from all over the world to pray and to place written prayers in the cracks of the huge foundation stones.

Wilderness Tabernacle- During the 40 years that Israel wandered in the wilderness after the Exodus, G_d dwelt among them, and they worshipped Him at the Tabernacle (also called the Tent of Meeting). This was a predecessor to the *First Temple* of Solomon. In Exodus 25ff, G_d defines to Moses specifically how His Tabernacle should be constructed and the specifics to the liturgy. In Exodus 40:34, after the construction was complete, G_d's *shekinah* glory enters the Tabernacle.

Yarmuk- Tributary river to the Jordan in the Golan Heights.

Yir'eh- '*Yir'eh*' generally means 'to see' or in a different verbal tense, to 'make one see something that was previously hidden'; but it can depending upon context also be glossed 'to provide' as in Gen 22:8 where Abraham tells Isaac that the Lord will 'provide' Himself the lamb.

Yom Kippur- The annual day (10th of Tishri) upon which the verdict of G_d upon all guilty mankind is issued from the Temple. It is also on this day when G_d provides the suitable substitute offering for the sin of the repentant. These rituals and offerings not only pay for the crimes of the repentant participants, but also purges the Temple from all sin residue that would cause G_d to hesitate blessing His people. It is on this day alone that the High Priest can enter the Holy of Holies to purge the sin residue from the Ark of Covenant. Also called the Day of Purgation, the Day of Atonement.

Zakkai- Rabbi Yochanan ben Zakkai, a student of Hillel was an important Jewish sage in the late *Second Temple* period. He miraculously avoided being killed with the other Jewish scholars in the Roman siege of Jerusalem in 70 AD. He gathered his disciples in Jamnia and began the process of identifying a post-Temple Judaism. He was an important contributor to the *Mishnah*.

---

[i] See Exodus 40:34-5 (NIV).
[ii] Psalm 93:1 (author's translation).
[iii] Psalm 93:2 (author's translation).
[iv] Psalm 93:3 (author's translation).
[v] Psalm 93:4 (author's translation).
[vi] Psalm 93:5 (author's translation).
[vii] See Psalm 98.
[viii] Psalm 98:1 (author's translation).
[ix] Psalm 98:2-3 (author's translation).
[x] Psalm 98:4 (author's translation).
[xi] Psalm 98:5 (author's translation).
[xii] Psalm 98:6a (author's translation).
[xiii] Psalm 98:6b-9 (author's translation).
[xiv] Recent archaeology has found evidence of a huge copper smelting complex in Jordan, on the Wadi Arabah some 30 miles from the Dead Sea and 30 miles north of Petra. The site Khirbat en-Nahas (lit. 'the ruins of copper') is near a series of deep copper mines and has been dated to have been active during the time of David and Solomon.
[xv] See Exodus 34:6-7 (JPS).
[xvi] See Numbers 29:1-6 (JPS).

[xvii] See Exodus 21:30, Lev 20:10, but see also Num 35:31-3.

[xviii] See Leviticus 6:1-7 (NIV)

[xix] See Psalm 107 (JPS)

[xx] Psalm 88:3-8 (NIV revised)

[xxi] See Numbers 15:30-31 (NIV).

[xxii] See Psalm 85:2-3 (JPS).

[xxiii] See Chaim Richman, *The Holy Temple of Jerusalem* (p. 53-5).

[xxiv] See Leviticus 16 for this (and particularly 16:16).

[xxv] See Chaim Richman, p. 53-5.

[xxvi] With sincere apologies to C.S. Lewis.

[xxvii] See Lev 16:29-30 (JPS).

[xxviii] See Psalm 122 (JPS).

[xxix] Psalm 98:1-3 (author's translation)

[xxx] See Gen 17:5 (NIV).

[xxxi] See Psalm 2 (JPS).

[xxxii] Psalm 2:10-12 (NIV).

[xxxiii] See Psalm 122 (NIV).

[xxxiv] See Psalm 133 (NIV).

[xxxv] See Psalm 118 (NIV).

[xxxvi] Psalm 118:6-7 (NIV)

[xxxvii] Psalm 118 (NIV)

[xxxviii] See Dt 17:14ff (NIV).

[xxxix] M. Hilkhot Teshuvah 3.4 as quoted in Reuven Hammer's very helpful book, *Entering the High Holy Days: A Complete Guide to the History, Prayers, and Themes*, (Philadelphia: The Jewish Publication Society, 1998) p. 71.

[xl] In *Avot derabbi natan-a*, 4 as quoted in Hammer, p. 14.

[xli] R. Hammer, *Entering the High Holy Days: A Complete Guide to the History, Prayers and Themes*, (Philadelphia: Jewish Publication Society, 1998), p. 5. See also M. Segal, "The Religion of Israel Before Sinai", *Jewish Quarterly Review* 52 (1963), 242-5, S. Mowinckel, *The Psalms in Israel's Worship, Vol 1* (Oxford, 1962), 120 ff.

7509222R0

Made in the USA
Charleston, SC
12 March 2011